DEVIL'S CANYON

Forensic Geography

THE CRIME SCENE CLUB: FACT AND FICTION

Devil's Canyon: Forensic Geography

Over the Edge: Forensic Accident Reconstruction

The Trickster's Image: Forensic Art

Poison and Peril: Forensic Toxicology

Close-Up: Forensic Photography

Face from the Past: Skull Reconstruction

The Monsoon Murder: Forensic Meteorology

If the Shoe Fits: Footwear Analysis

The Earth Cries Out: Forensic Chemistry and Environmental Science

Things Fall Apart: Forensic Engineering

Numbering the Crime: Forensic Mathematics

A Stranger's Voice: Forensic Speech

DEVIL'S CANYON

Forensic Geography

Kenneth McIntosh

Mason Crest Publishers

DEVIL'S CANYON: FORENSIC GEOGRAPHY

MASON CREST PUBLISHERS INC.
370 Reed Road
Broomall, Pennsylvania 19008
(866)MCP-BOOK (toll free)
www.masoncrest.com

First Printing

9 8 7 6 5 4 3 2 1

978-1-4222-0259-3 (set)

Library of Congress Cataloging-in-Publication Data

McIntosh, Kenneth, 1959–
Devil's canyon : forensic geography / by Kenneth McIntosh.
p. cm. — (The Crime Scene Club ; case #1)
Includes bibliographical references.
ISBN 978-1-4222-0247-0 ISBN 978-1-4222-1450-3
[1. Criminal investigation—Fiction. 2. Forensic sciences—Fiction. 3. Mystery and detective stories.] I. Title.
PZ7.M1858De 2009
[Fic]—dc22

2008033235

Design by MK Bassett-Harvey.
Produced by Harding House Publishing Service, Inc.
www.hardinghousepages.com
Cover design by MK Bassett-Harvey.
Cover and interior illustrations by Justin Miller.
Printed in Malaysia.

CONTENTS

INTRODUCTION

The sound of breaking glass. A scream. A shot. Then . . . silence. Blood, fingerprints, a bullet, a skull, fire debris, a hair, shoeprints—enter the wonderful world of forensic science. A world of searching to find clues, collecting that which others cannot see, testing to find answers to seemingly impossible questions, and testifying to juries so that justice will be served. A world where curiosity, love of a puzzle, and gathering information are basic. The books in this series will take you to this world.

The CSI Effect

The TV show *CSI: Crime Scene Investigator* became so widely popular that *CSI: Miami* and *CSI: NY* followed. This forensic interest spilled over into *Bones* (anthropology); *Crossing Jordan* and *Dr. G* (medical examiners); *New Detectives* and *Forensic Files*, which cover all the forensic disciplines. Almost every modern detective story now involves forensic science. Many fiction books are written, some by forensic scientists such as Kathy Reichs (anthropology) and Ken Goddard (criminalistics and crime scene), as well as textbooks such as *Criminalistics* by Richard Saferstein. Other crime fiction authors are Sir Arthur Conan Doyle (Sherlock Holmes), Thomas Harris (*Red Dragon*), Agatha Christie (Hercule Poirot) and Ellis Peters, whose hero is a monk, Cadfael, an ex-Crusader who solves crimes. The list goes on and on—and I encourage you to read them all!

The spotlight on forensic science has had good *and* bad effects, however. Because the books and TV shows are so enjoyable, the limits of science have been blurred to make the plots more interesting. Often when students are intrigued by the TV shows and want to learn more, they have a rude awakening. The crime scene investigators on TV do the work of many professionals, including police officers, medical examiners, forensic laboratory scientists, anthropologists, and entomologists, to mention just a few. And all this in addition to processing crime scenes! Fictional instruments give test results at warp speed, and crimes are solved in forty-two minutes. Because of the overwhelming popularity of these shows, juries now expect forensic evidence in every case.

The books in this series will take you to both old and new forensic sciences, perhaps tweaking your interest in a career. If so, take courses in chemistry, biology, math, English, public speaking, and drama. Get a summer job in a forensic laboratory, courthouse, law enforcement agency, or an archeological dig. Seek internships and summer jobs (even unpaid). Skills in microscopy, instrumentation, and logical thinking will help you. Curiosity is a definite plus. You must read and understand procedures; take good notes; calculate answers; and prepare solutions. Public speaking and/or drama courses will make you a better speaker and a better expert witness. The ability to write clear, understandable reports aimed at nonscientists is a must. Salaries vary across the country and from agency to agency. You will never get rich, but you will have a satisfying, interesting career.

So come with me into this wonderful world called forensic science. You will be intrigued and entertained. These books are awesome!

—Carla M. Noziglia MS, FAAFS

Prologue
1896

"Don't talk to strangers. Bad things could happen to a little girl alone on this train."

"I'll be careful, Mama."

Felicity Hudson slid out of the seat beside her mother, straightened her pinafore, and started down the aisle, headed to the dining car for a penny candy. The iron horse lurched from side to side, keeping her slightly off balance. The carriage reeked with an unsavory mix of cologne, perfume, cigar smoke, and whisky.

In all her eight years, she had never before been west of the Mississippi, nor had she ridden a train. This trip across the continent to visit her aunt in California was the kind of adventure she had only imagined from dime novels.

The passenger car swayed and she grabbed the side of the bench next to her for support, then snatched away her hand, realizing she had touched a cold steel tube. She stared, gape-jawed. A real six-shooter! Its nickel-plated barrel extended downward until it reached the top of a man's polished leather boot.

"My, aren't you the pretty little one?" The gruff voice froze Felicity. "Care for a piece of beef jerky?"

She lifted her gaze, up past the silk vest, gold watch chain, and badge, past the red scarf around a weathered neck, up to a craggy face and handlebar mustache. The man looked down at her with cold grey eyes. Trembling, she backed away, her gaze locked on the stranger, until she reached the end of the train, where she turned and pushed open the door.

The cool wind refreshed her spirits as she grasped the railing and watched the scenery rush by. She loved to stand outside between the carriages, but Mama wouldn't allow it, so Felicity made every excuse she could to go back and forth to the diner, pausing as long as she could between cars.

Her reverie was interrupted by an enormous crash and screech as the train came to a violent halt. The entire world seemed to turn upside down. Felicity flew sidewise, over the railing and onto the sand. Tremors shook the ground like the aftermath of an earthquake. As dust settled around her, she gazed in shock at the train. Ahead, the engine lay on its side.

She was about to stand and shake the dust off her dress, when she heard a sound behind her: horses, at a gallop. She crawled toward the train, just in time to escape being trampled under the hooves of four steeds. Feeling as though she had stumbled into a nightmare, she stared up at the riders' rushing blurred shapes, dark against the sun, their eyes shaded under wide-brimmed hats.

Ka-boom! The explosion echoed off the walls of the canyon as an orange plume shot out from the side of the freight car.

She hid beneath the engine, crouching behind a wheel. From this shelter, she heard the crunch of boots on the sand, and looked out at three men striding by her hiding place. Each one carried a drawn gun, and one she recognized as the grey-eyed stranger who had spoken to her on the train.

There was a strange, hushed moment of eerie calm—and then a man's voice spoke, loud and stern: "Hold it right there! Drop yer irons."

Silence.

"I said drop 'em. Hurry up and no one gets hurt."

A quick shuffling sound and then— *Shunk!*

A bullet slammed into the wood above Felicity's head. She closed her eyes and shook.

"They got Tex!" It was a voice she hadn't heard before.

"We knew there'd be guards. Tex took his chances like the rest of us. Now get in that car and start hauling out loot."

"But aintcha gonna do something 'bout Tex?"

"All I'm gonna do is hope mercy's in business when he reaches the pearly gates. He'll need it. Now, move it. José's already in that car packing loot. Get busy and join him before I draw this iron again."

Lured by curiosity, Felicity inched out from behind the wheel and peered ahead. Three forms lay still on the ground, a couple of yards out from the train. Horses stood waiting next to the freight car. Then, three men emerged from the side of the car, carrying bulging burlap pouches. They loaded these into the saddle bags.

"Hurry up!" The lead robber shouted. "Move those bags fast and let's get outta here."

"Hey, Boss?" It was a third man, who spoke with a Spanish accent.

"What?"

"Want me to put some more slugs in those Pinkerton men? They might not be dead."

"Nah, save your ammo."

"But—"

"Doggone it, do what I say! We've gotta get moving now. You know we have to reach the cave and stash all this loot before sundown."

"Hey-ah!"

"Gidda-yup!"

With a clatter of hooves, the three bandits swept past Felicity and disappeared round a bend in the canyon.

She stood up on shaky legs, gasped for air, glanced toward the dead men, and screamed. One of the corpses was sitting up.

It was the gray-eyed man who had spoken to her. He looked at the girl and blinked.

"You a ghost?" she quavered.

"Derned near to one. I'm amazed to be alive." The man's hat had fallen off, and he rubbed at the side of his head. "Bullet grazed me, I guess. Got knocked out cold. Just now came to and missed all a' the action."

He stared at the bodies of his companions. "Poor fellas, they died doin' their duty, guardin' that safe. All for nothin'."

"Who—who were those men?"

"Haven't seen 'em before, so I couldn't tell you. Good for nothin' train robbers is all I know. They're at least a mile east of here by now, and it'll take half

an hour to get a posse together to trail 'em. Looks like they've gotten away."

"My baby!"

Felicity suddenly felt her mother's soft arms lifting her. "Oh, thank heavens you're all right!" her mother whispered in her ear.

Felicity dropped her head against her mother's breast and burst into tears.

Chapter 1
CRIME SCENE CLUB

Lupe stared at the egg burrito on the plate in front of her. Her little brother Hector made a rude noise and wiggled his tongue. She was not amused.

"*Mija*, eat your breakfast," her mother urged.

Lupe scrunched her nose, focused on a piece of ham lurking in its bed of cheese and chorizo, and felt queasy.

"What's the matter, *Niña*?"

"I'm not a child. Don't call me that."

"Your mother is only trying to help you. Don't be testy," her dad admonished.

"I'm gonna' be fat if I eat all this. No one likes a fat girl."

"Fat? Why look at you, *Flaca*. Not an ounce of meat on your bones."

Lupe glanced up from her plate at her mother. Mom wore a white tank-top, her long black hair hanging loose over the shoulders. Her face was round, kind but aging. Lupe's namesake, the Virgin of Guadalupe, adorned her mother's left shoulder in tattooed shades of red and blue; a heart with her name, Yolanda, and her father's name, Raul, curled around her right bicep. *Why can't she at least wear longer sleeves, so her tattoos wouldn't show?* Lupe loved her mom, but she didn't like to be seen with her in public.

She sighed. "Mama, when you and Dad were sweethearts in the '80s things were different. Your *pachuca* friends didn't mind a bit of extra weight. But we're not in the *barrio*—we're in Flagstaff. People look healthy here. And have you seen the models in fashion magazines lately?"

"*Sí*, they're skinny as rails. Sick looking chicas."

"Awful role models," her dad added.

Lupe decided it was time to change the subject. "I'll be home late tonight, around five."

Her mother's eyebrows went up.

"Remember? I told you, this is the first meeting for Crime Scene Club, after school."

"Oh, sí, sí."

"Hey Dad, are you going to pick up that flat-screen TV from Wal-Mart today?" Lupe had been waiting anxiously to see all her favorite crime shows in high definition.

There was a long, unexpected pause. Yolanda and Raul glanced at each other.

"Is there a problem?"

"*Mija*, we've been waiting for the right time to tell you," her mom replied. "We're not getting the new TV. They've cut my hours at work so we can't afford it, and . . . they might lay me off if things don't get better soon."

"Won't we do okay with Dad's work?"

"Sorry, Lupe," her father replied. "They don't pay much for custom car painting in Flagstaff. In fact,

I've been making some calls to old friends where we used to live, to see if they know of any work."

"What? You're not thinking of moving back there." A glance at her father's face confirmed Lupe's worst fear. "I hate that city."

"Lupe, we have to do what's best for *la familia.* It's so expensive living here, and it's hard to find work that pays good."

"No." Lupe jumped up, grabbed her jacket and backpack off the counter. "I'm not moving back there. I hate that place."

"*Mija*, wait—"

But Lupe was already dashing through the door. It banged shut behind her, and she took a deep breath, then strode down the sidewalk toward the shortcut that led to school through the woods.

The chill morning air cooled her anger. She watched the little puffs of dragons' breath that came and went from her mouth as she walked. Ponderosa pines lined the trail, pointing straight upward into the fog. The San Francisco Peaks loomed invisibly behind the mist, the vast backdrop to her life in Flagstaff.

In the city where Lupe used to live, the air was as brown as the washed-out houses. Tweakers and prostitutes hung out in the streets. She shivered, not just from the cold. *God, if you're answering prayers today, please don't make me move back there.*

After a long, dreary day of classes, the end-of-the-day bell clanged, and students streamed out of the classrooms of Flagstaff Charter School. Lupe stashed books in her locker, then headed toward room B1, where the Crime Scene Club was going to hold its first meeting. Thank heavens there was something to look forward to before going home.

Inside Mr. Chesterton's science classroom stood long tables with stools and glass beakers; pictures of galaxies and forests hung on the walls.

"Hello, Lupe." Mr. C was a big man, in girth and in height, with a red beard and shoulder-length hair, like a carrot-top Santa Claus. He was the school's instructor for the new group. Lupe pulled out a stool, sat and waited, eager to meet her companions in this new endeavor.

When the door opened, a girl she recognized from study hall entered. She wore an ankle-length black overcoat, and her dark hair was piled on her head like a crazy bird's nest. Piercings adorned her nose and one eyebrow. *SHE's in Crime Scene Club?*

Again, the door swung open, and this time a couple came in: a Native American boy and a girl with blond dreadlocks. As the newcomers seated themselves beside Lupe at the long table, another student walked in: a thin boy with pale skin and John Lennon spectacles. He was carrying a laptop computer, which he set on the table and immediately opened. Without glancing at the others, he began poking at the keys, his fingers flying. The last to enter was an Asian-American woman, sharply dressed in business jacket and skirt. She whisked into the room and flashed a trained smile at the students.

The science teacher cleared his throat. "Welcome to Crime Scene Club. I'm already proud of each of you—you five were chosen from more than forty applicants." He beamed.

The girl dressed in black whispered in Lupe's ear, "They must've been on crack if we're the cream of the crop."

Mr. Chesterton motioned to the woman beside him. "This is Ms. Kwan, our club representative, a detective with the Flagstaff Police Department."

"Good afternoon," the police woman stepped forward. "As you know, this club is part of the Adopt-A-School program. We've decided to make some of our advanced forensic equipment available for you to use, and we're going to enlist your help in real crime cases. This is an experiment—and in some ways it's controversial. But we are sure you'll be very responsible and we hope this club will be a success."

She's sure or she hopes? Lupe wondered. Ms. Kwan impressed her as the kind of person who masks hidden insecurities by acting extra self-confident.

The door opened again behind Ms. Kwan, and a man in casual business dress, entered. *Looks like Brad Pitt,* Lupe thought. The handsome stranger took his place at the front of the room. "Sorry I'm late. I had to finish installing a system for a client."

"No problem," Mr. Chesterton replied. "Class, this is—"

"Bob McGinnis," the man interjected. "I represent Safe West Security Systems. We're honored to be the financial sponsor for your new club, and if your parents need a security plan for their home or

business, I hope you'll tell them to call Safe West." He smiled broadly.

"He can do my system any day," the girl beside Lupe whispered and rolled her pierced tongue around darkened lips.

"Okay," Ms. Kwan said, "are you students ready to hear about our first case? I understand some of you have met Stanley Peshlaki." Lupe had; he was a Navajo *haatali*, or medicine man, and also an artist. He came to their school occasionally to share his knowledge of local plants and their healing properties, or to give tips on painting. Ms. Kwan continued, "Mr. Peshlaki lives just outside Flagstaff, near the Navajo Nation. Yesterday, around seven a.m., Mr. Peshlaki was awakened by a thud on his door. When he answered, no one was there, but a written death threat lay on the ground, tied to a rock. Our first case is to find out who wrote that note, and make sure Mr. Peshlaki is safe from harm."

"But, before we go any further," said Mr. Chesterton, "Ms. Kwan and Mr. McGinnis want to get to know all of you. So let's take a minute and tell us your names, hobbies, and why you tried out for this club." He motioned to the handsome boy at the end of the table. "Ken, you start."

"Okay, uh, hello everyone. My name is Ken Benally. I'm a senior this year. I'm on the school soccer team, and I play guitar with a band—Red, White, and Blues, we're playing Friday at Below the Tracks Club—feel free to come see us. I got into forensic science because my dad's a sergeant in the Police Department and it's cool." Lupe noted the calm, controlled way Ken presented himself, and she wondered if he was attached to the girl with the dreads. "Okay, it's your turn, Jessa." Ken turned to the girl beside him.

"Hey, I'm Jessa Carter. I'm a junior. I'm totally into blues and roots music. I sing, play guitar, paint.

. . . The reason I applied for Crime Scene Club is because there's something really cool about crime, you know? It's that whole gritty noir thing, yeah?"

"Cosmic, baby," the girl in black mimicked.

Jessa appeared undaunted. "Oh, and my man on bass guitar"—she rubbed her hand on Ken's shoulder—"thought I should be part of this gig, too."

Now it was Lupe's turn to introduce her self. "Hello. My name is Guadalupe Rosa Mendez Arellano, but you can just call me Lupe. I'm a junior, and I love to read, especially crime stories and westerns. When I was a little girl a teacher handed me a Nancy Drew paperback and I've been hooked on mysteries ever since. That's basically why I'm here."

She nodded toward the girl next to her. "Your turn." *Time for the freak show*.

The girl in black gave a deep sigh. "I'm Maeve Murphy. I'm a junior—stinks, but wait 'til next year when I get even. I'm into gothic horror, psycho movies. . . . Yeah, well, I had to join some sorta organization 'cause my mom's bugging me, and this was the only one that had to do with death and violence. So, you're gonna have to deal with me. Your turn, dork." She turned to the blonde-haired boy.

Lupe noted how the smiles on the faces of the adults in the room had gradually faded as Maeve did her introduction. Now the spectacled boy spoke in an emotionless monotone, still typing into his keyboard. "Everyone I know calls me Wire. I could tell you my birth name but you're all supposed to be smart, so you can figure it out for yourselves, and if you can't manage that, you don't belong here. I do computer programming and play RPG online, professionally. I joined this club because it's the only way I can use the advanced programs that Flagstaff police have for crime investigation and because all the classes here are so lame. I'm hoping this club will provide some intellectual challenge."

The look on Ms. Kwan's face made Lupe hide a smile. "Ah, okay," the detective said. "You're a very, uh, unusual group and that could, um, potentially be helpful in solving crimes." She took a breath. "This first meeting, we want to introduce you to some of the basics of forensics history and philosophy."

"Great," Maeve whispered, "like another class."

Mr. Chesterton grabbed an erasable marker and stood by the whiteboard. "I know history may not be your favorite subject, but you'll appreciate forensics more if you understand its origins. Basically, two Frenchmen in the nineteenth century founded our modern methods of crime detection." He wrote on the board the names "Eugene Vidocq" and "Edmond Locard."

"The French invented something besides fries?" Wire whispered.

"Of course! Remember Monet, Renoir, Cezanne?" Jessa responded.

"Don't forget French kisses," Maeve smirked.

Lupe glared at them. Is anyone in this club going to take it seriously?

The science teacher continued, oblivious to the whispers. "In his youth, Vidocq was a criminal and a jail-breaker. But he went on to invent the basics of criminal investigation. He began the study of ballistics, criminal record-keeping, casting footprints, and even the profession we call 'private investigator.'" The instructor pointed to the other name on the board. "Locard, the other founder of scientific crime investigation, was known as the Sherlock Holmes of France. He was the first person to state the most important principle of forensics. Anyone know what that is?"

"Stopping for coffee and donuts?" Maeve suggested.

Lupe shot her hand up. "Every contact leaves a trace."

"Excellent!"

"Hey, just a moment." Wire looked up from his laptop. "That isn't true."

"No?"

"Crimes often happen without a trace. You get a really good criminal, someone familiar with forensic science, and he can cover his tracks perfectly. If I were going to commit some crime, I would alter the evidence of entry, wipe down all the surfaces I touched, then mop the floors and vacuum the carpet. There are plenty of smart criminals. That's why more than one in three murders goes unpunished. The right person can commit a crime and leave no more evidence than a ghost."

"Yes," Mr. Chesterton agreed, "but that doesn't mean he hasn't left some trace. It just isn't discernible. The motion of a butterfly's wings leaves some influence on the movement of the earth's atmosphere, but it's so slight we're unaware of it. Likewise, even the best criminal will leave some sort of clue—and the challenge to forensic science is to get better and better, until we can detect the tiniest traces of evidence."

Lupe was intrigued. "What if we can't find a physical clue? Then the criminal gets away?"

"Not necessarily," Ms. Kwan entered the discussion. "Some forms of criminal science don't depend so heavily on physical evidence. You might be familiar with mathematical profiling—there's a popular TV show about that. And there's a technique that we're excited about at Flagstaff PD. Have you ever heard of geographical profiling?"

"It's the study of patterns and places in multiple, connected crimes," answered Wire. "You start with the crime scene, then work backward, using the linkage of crime location and physical boundaries to establish a jeopardy surface, revealing the criminal's residence or staging area for the crime."

"In English, please?" Maeve retorted.

"By studying the location of several crimes, we can sometimes guess where the next crime is likely to occur," Ms. Kwan explained.

"They've had amazing success with that in Canada," Ken added. "In one case, a serial rapist was tracked down to his basement hideout, purely by computer analysis of crime locations."

Ms. Kwan nodded. "You two are really up on things. We have a new piece of equipment at FPD, called a 'total station,' that takes a highly accurate spatial record of a crime scene, and a computer program called Predator, to help us analyze multiple, connected crimes. Of course, we don't haul them out for every little case—but in bigger crimes they're great tools to have."

"Cool," Wire said. "We can solve cases from our computers."

"Not entirely," Mr. Chesterton corrected. "These new, advanced technologies are helpful, but they don't substitute for basic crime scene work. You'll first learn to secure a site, then leave a site undisturbed and look for the very smallest traces of physical evidence like fingerprints, hairs, fibers, blood spots, and so on. You'll have to thoroughly document a crime scene. When investigating, we have to pursue every possible angle. Something that seems insignificant—like whether a door is opened or shut—can be important for a case. When the perpetrator is finally brought to the courtroom, he won't be convicted on the basis of profiling. Prosecutors need hard, physical evidence to keep criminals off the street. So at a crime scene, we leave no stone unturned. After we do the basic work, then you can get to your computer analysis, Wire."

"I thought this club was going to be fun," Maeve grumbled. "Sounds like an awful lot of work."

She said it under her breath, but Ms. Kwan apparently had sharp ears. "I don't think 'fun' is the right word—a detective has to deal with harsh realities, and most of us are in therapy at one time or another. But this work can be"—she searched for the right word—"exhilarating. There's a rush you get when you find that vital clue. Maybe that's why fictional detective Sherlock Holmes took drugs when he didn't have a case. He had a hard time living without the thrill of crime scene work."

"So this could be as good as drugs? Guess I'm stickin' with this club," Maeve declared.

"One more thing." Mr. Chesterton was trying to get his lesson back on track. "Always expect the unexpected."

"That doesn't make sense, either," Wire protested.

"Yes it does," Jessa argued. "He's saying it's as much an art as a science, right Mr. C?"

"That's the idea," the teacher agreed.

Ms. Kwan concluded the meeting. "We'll begin our first case with a field trip to Mr. Peshlaki's place. I'll introduce you to the basics of examining a crime scene: interviewing, photographing, and collecting material evidence. We'll also learn about the physical setting of the crime, so if necessary we can map the case. We leave tomorrow as soon as school lets out. Here are permission slips for the trip. Your parents will have to sign or you won't be allowed to go."

Lupe pulled on her jacket and headed quickly out the door. From forty applications the school came up with this group? She fingered the permission slip in her pocket, unsure whether she should bother having her parents sign it.

Chapter 2
DEVIL'S CANYON

Lupe debated overnight whether she would continue with Crime Scene Club. At breakfast she asked her dad to sign the field-trip permission form, but she was still unsure whether to go or not.

During lunchtime, she wandered behind the school and sat beneath a piñon tree, disinterested in food or company. She heard a rustle, and looked up to see Ken Benally leaning against a branch beside her.

"Mr. C says you haven't turned in your slip yet. You going on the trip?"

Why do you care? "My dad signed the form," she said out loud, "but I'm not sure. Crime Scene Club is . . . not what I expected."

"Weird bunch, huh?"

"Yeah."

"Well," Ken hesitated a moment, then went on, "I hope you go on the trip. I'd like . . . it would be nice to get to know you better."

She looked into his face. Was it just friendliness she saw there, or a different sort of attraction? She decided to stick with the club—at least for the time being.

Hours later, Crime Scene Club was packed into a white SUV, bumping along a winding dirt road. Mr. C was at the wheel, negotiating the twists and turns. Ms. Kwan sat shotgun, talking over her shoulder to the teens in back. In the middle seat, Lupe and Jessa were seated by the windows, with Ken in the middle. Jessa had placed her hand on Ken's, Lupe noted, yet Ken shot frequent glances at Lupe. Wire and Maeve sat in the back seat.

"It's important to understand the location of a crime," Ms. Kwan was explaining. "Forensic science is a lot like journalism: your job is to figure out the who, where, when, what, and why of a situation. And the *where* is especially important here in Northern Arizona, where people and place are so closely intertwined."

The car hit a bump that jolted all its occupants. Lupe's hand came down accidentally on Ken's leg. He looked at her and smiled, then turned to face Jessa, who glared at the other girl.

Ms. Kwan continued, "This area is called Devil's Canyon. It's not well known like the Grand Canyon, but it's still impressive. The bottom is an arroyo—that is, a mostly dry riverbed. Viewed from the air, the canyon looks like an enormous centipede, almost a hundred miles long, crawling from northeast to southwest with countless small tributaries extending outward. If a man wanted to hide out here, he could evade searchers for many months—especially if he knows the land well. Notice that we have to go a long distance out of our way on this road that loops around and then descends to the floor. It's important to note topography when looking at crime scenes, because victims and criminals all have to deal with the same barriers and access routes."

The car jolted violently again, as if to underscore the officer's words. "You should also understand the history of a site," Ms. Kwan went on. "This is ancestral hunting and raiding grounds for the Navajo and Apache tribes, going back at least seven hundred years. And in 1896, a famous train robbery took place near the site we're visiting today. I have an article, reprinted from the *Northern Sun* newspaper, the day after the event."

Ms. Kwan passed out copies and Lupe read:

Train Robbed—Fortune in Gold and Silver Missing.
March 14, 1896, Flagstaff Arizona.

Yesterday, when the Atchison, Topeka and Santa Fe Railroad failed to arrive for its afternoon stop at the Flagstaff station, the sheriff and a posse, accompanied by our reporter, set out east along the track. They found the train, derailed, at the point where it crosses

through Devil's Canyon. At 2:10 PM the engine crashed and derailed after it hit a section of rail removed by saboteurs. Moments later, four armed assailants blasted open the freight car, blowing open a locked safe in the process.

The safe was guarded by three agents of the Pinkerton agency, who were riding in the passenger car when the train derailed. They confronted the robbers and shot it out, killing one of the outlaws but losing two of their number. A third Pinkerton man, known as Big Jake M (name protected), was knocked out by a bullet but regained consciousness shortly after the lethal exchange. Big Jake is well known in Texas for apprehending rustlers, and killing a notorious desperado with his long-barreled Colt Buntline revolver.

The safe contained half a million in recently minted silver dollars and gold bars, property of the Pacific Coast Cattleman's Bank, being transferred from their Albuquerque branch to San Francisco. The robbers appear to have escaped with the entire fortune.

The closest witness to the crime was a young girl, Felicity H, who was thrown off the train when it crashed. She hid under a carriage and overheard the shootout and discussion between thieves. They declared they would reach a cave and hide the treasure before nightfall. When he came to, Big Jake commented to this girl that the robbers had already gone too far east for capture. Authorities have been unable to identify the thieves. Their hoof prints disappeared in a flooded section of the arroyo.

"Did anyone ever find the gold?" Ken asked.

Ms. Kwan shook her head. "Not a cent."

"The robbers?"

"Disappeared from history."

The winding road leveled onto the canyon floor, briefly ran alongside the arroyo, and then came to a small, green valley west of the canyon. Mr. C. stopped the engine.

As the club climbed out of the car, Ms. Kwan went around to the back gate of the SUV and took out a large plastic container.

"Crime scene kit?" asked Ken.

"Yep."

"What's in it?" Jessa inquired.

"Tape, flashlight, a notebook with pens, paper sacks, rubber bands, disposable mask and gloves, a tape measure, fingerprinting equipment, a field test to detect blood and drugs."

"Wow, everything but the kitchen sink."

"This is a very basic kit." Ms. Kwan replied. "Are any of you skilled at photography?" The detective held up an expensive-looking digital camera and extending lens.

"I am," both Lupe and Jessa replied simultaneously.

"Here Jessa, you take this. I'll tell you what to shoot, and how to set the camera."

Lupe thought the blonde girl shot her a smug smile, but she tried to take her mind off Jessa by focusing instead on her surroundings. At the side of the alcove, under a huge red rock overhang, was Stanley Peshlaki's house, a traditional eight-sided log and earth Hogan. A tin chimney stuck out from the top, but an array of modern solar panels stood beside the ancient-styled home. Beside the door of the dwelling was an artist's easel. A flock of several dozen sheep grazed near the dwelling, and a rough wooden corral next to the Hogan held half a dozen horses.

"*Yaateh.* Welcome," an old but sprightly man called out, opening the door of the Hogan.

"Hello, Mr. Peshlaki," Ms. Kwan responded. "This is the Crime Scene Club, the group I told you about when I called." She introduced each of the teens, and Mr. Peshlaki invited them inside.

The students took a seat on the couch or sat on pillows on the floor. Lupe glanced around at the décor: bright paintings of the canyon and of Navajo spiritual themes covered every wall. A woodstove stood in the middle of the room, with two small logs providing heat on this chilly afternoon. Bundles of herbs lay on a new television and DVD player. On a small chest of drawers, Lupe noted the haatali's cell phone, one the slim models. In the corner, she noted a rifle and scope beside several boxes of ammunition.

"Now, Mr. Peshlaki, tell us about this threatening note you received," the detective asked.

"Well, morning before yesterday, around seven, I heard this clunk on the door." Peshlaki spoke softly, clipping his words at the end. "When I pulled on my jeans and went outside, I found this—tied to a rock." He held up a piece of paper.

"Can you show us exactly where it was located outside the door?"

"Sure."

"Good. Jessa, before we leave, make sure you get a picture of the ground just outside the entrance, and we'll place a marker at the exact place Mr. Peshlaki found that note. Do you still have the rock and string, Mr. Peshlaki?"

The medicine man nodded and held the objects toward the detective. She pulled a pair of latex gloves out of her suit jacket, snapped them on, and placed both objects in a bag, which she labeled with a permanent marker. "And now," Ms. Kwan said, "may I see the threatening letter?"

Stanley Peshlaki handed the detective a piece of paper, folded in quarters. She unfolded it and turned it over. One side was a mass-produced target, with neatly printed lettering, "25 yards pistol." There were three holes in the bull's-eye.

".45 caliber," Ken murmured. Ms. Kwan nodded.

Turning over the paper, the detective read out loud, "Indian, move now. Or this will be you." There was a rude sketch of a man, apparently intended to represent Mr. Peshlaki, with the bullet holes perforating his forehead.

"Scary." Lupe met the old man's dark eyes.

"That's nothing, it's what happened this morning that frightens me," the medicine man replied.

Ms. Kwan bagged the threatening note, jotted a quick but precise label on the paper container, and explained, "We'll go over this with a chemical agent, looking for fingerprints. We'll also inspect it with a microscope for hairs or fibers. Finally, we'll apply ESDA."

"And for those of us who don't speak acronym?" Maeve asked.

"Electrostatic detection apparatus. It finds impressions made on a paper beneath other surfaces. We can find traces of writing in a notepad twenty pages deep using this device. But now," she turned to the Navajo artist, "you were saying something frightened you this morning?"

Stanley Peshlaki's wrinkled face seem to sag with grief. "When I went out, I found my sheepdog, Shadow, dead on the ground. He was getting old—he's been a wonderful companion for fourteen years—and I thought maybe he just passed away in his sleep. But then I looked a little closer and saw the red spot behind his ear. It was a bullet hole.

Someone killed Shadow, and I'd guess it's the same man who wrote that letter."

"That's awful," Jessa cried.

"Is Shadow's body where the killer left it?" asked Detective Kwan.

"Nope. When I came by there again, a few hours later, his body was gone. The coyotes or maybe a mountain lion took it. That's the way nature works," the old man replied.

"That's a shame. We could have learned something from the slug. But we'll examine the place where the body lay. Blood traces on the ground or grass will help us locate the direction of the shot. We'll also photograph the surrounding area and mark exact coordinates. It may be useful to place the spot on a computer map. Mr. Peshlaki, did you see any footprints around the place, this morning or the morning before yesterday?"

"No. The ground is rocky, so it's hard to find tracks—and I'm pretty good at sighting 'em. Some plants were pushed down, near the path that leads up through the canyon to the north, so I figure whoever did these things came and went that way."

"We'll document that. We may be able to discern the person's stride or maybe even shoe size from trampled vegetation. Have you seen any strangers around here lately?"

"One—a man on an ATV who drove into the valley here a week ago. I was outside painting—it was a sunny day—so I waved hello. He just glared at me, though, and went back the way he came."

"What did he look like?"

"He was a ways away, but he had a white cowboy hat, long-sleeved shirt, and bolo tie."

"Have you seen him since?"

"No."

"Anyone else around lately?"

"Just Joe, the homeless guy. Don't know his last name. He's been camping around here for the past six weeks or so. Doesn't ever talk much, keeps to himself, but he's never hurt anyone that I know of. We wave whenever we see each other, then go our own ways."

Lupe knew Joe; he hung around downtown Flagstaff for a few days each month, occasionally stopping at Café Paradiso Coffee Shop, where Lupe worked. He said little, acted eccentric, but she had always assumed he was harmless.

Ms. Kwan led the group outside, and they spent the next few hours documenting the area. She explained to the students how to walk carefully and avoid contaminating a site by adding footprints or tramping over tiny clues.

Jessa took numerous photos, including close-ups of the places where the note and murdered dog were found, as well as longer-range pictures of Mr. Peshlaki's dwelling, the valley, and adjacent trails. The detective explained to Jessa how to adjust the camera settings to get high-resolution, sharp impressions of the trampled vegetation near the trailhead, the blood spots where the dog had been shot, and other details.

At Ms. Kwan's request, Wire took readings with a global positioning satellite receiver, coordinated those with the pictures that Jessa took, and recorded the data on his computer. "All these pictures and readings are useless if we can't put the pieces of the puzzle together back at the lab," the detective explained. "Documentation may be the most crucial part of an investigation. One little omission—failure to record a picture or piece of evidence—may allow a criminal to walk free on a technicality. I've seen it happen."

"The Hardy Boys never worked this hard on a case," Ken whispered to Jessa.

"Hey! Look." Lupe pointed to a small cactus near the place where Shadow had died.

"I don't see anything," Maeve said.

"I do." Jessa focused the close-up lens on the place where Lupe was pointing. "A couple of fibers . . . that cactus caught someone's clothes."

"Excellent!" Ms. Kwan smiled. "This is how we do crime scene work." She took out a tiny bag and tweezers to carefully bag the tiny fibers. Maeve stuck out her tongue at the other two girls.

As the sun began to set, the CSC teens loaded Ms. Kwan's gear back into the truck. Then they stepped back into the medicine man's dwelling to say good-bye. "We'll keep tight on this case," the policewoman promised Mr. Peshlaki. "Please be very careful. Anyone that can shoot a pet like that. . ." The detective glanced at the teens and looked worried. Lupe wondered if Ms. Kwan was sorry she had involved the club with this case.

"I'm looking out for myself." The old man glanced toward the rifle and ammunition in the corner. "My family has dealt with troublemakers wanting us off this land for five centuries. I'll be okay."

As they drove away from the Hogan, Lupe looked back at the medicine man standing outside his home. He looked very small and alone, she thought.

The detective put her hand on the girl's shoulder. "I'm sorry for your loss. Believe me, I'll do right by your friend."

Jessa nodded and blinked back fresh tears. Then she got up and headed for her mother's car. Once she was out of sight of the mansion, she parked and leaned her head on the wheel. There was no need to fight her tears any longer.

It was eleven-thirty by the time Jessa got home, but she didn't feel tired yet. She sat in her room, strumming her guitar; Ken and Carlos were the real musicians in their band, but she could do chords and often played the guitar for her private enjoyment. Tonight she sung the mournful words of an old tune: "Fare you well, fare you well, I loved you more than words can tell."

When she was crying too hard to sing any longer, she put down her guitar and pulled her journal out of the drawer by her bed.

Chapter 3
DARK ALLEY

The following evening, Café Paradiso Coffee Shop was filled with customers, sipping their lattés and chais, playing chess, working on their laptops, or just shooting the breeze. Lupe flew from table to table.

"Can I get you more coffee?"

"I'll bring the check whenever you're ready."

"I'll be right back with your order."

She noticed a customer wearing a crumpled hiking cap, his back to her. "Evening, sir. Can I take your order?"

The man turned to face her; unkempt hair and beard framed a face as weathered as the sides of a desert canyon. One eye focused on her, while the other seemed to drift sideways, eerily independent of its counterpart.

Lupe sucked in her breath. "Hi, Joe. In town for a couple days?"

"Yeah. Cold and foggy." He pointed outside the window. "Sleeping by the vents in town."

"I'm sorry, that must be uncomfortable."

He chuckled, a little longer than seemed appropriate. "Live my own way, beats enslavement by so-called civilization. But I'm rich tonight—so get me one of those fancy coffees the city folks drink."

"Do you want a latté, cappuccino, mocha, espresso. . . ?"

"How should I know? All those French words don't mean nothin' to me. Just get me what the rich folks drink."

"How about a double mocha with crème?"

"Fine. Fetch it."

She went behind the counter to prepare the drink.

"Hey Lupe, come here a minute," Sunshine Daydream, the owner of the coffee shop, called from the back.

"Need something?" Lupe stuck her head in the door of the back kitchen.

"Here." Sunshine handed Lupe a plate with a pasty mass on it. "I just whipped this up in the kitchen, special for you. It's soy bean and tofu mix, with crushed alfalfa sprouts and boysenberry topping."

"Gee . . . thanks Sunshine, no one's ever fixed anything like that for me before."

Lupe set the plate down, delivered Joe's drink, and then slipped out the rear of the restaurant into the alley. It was freezing outside, foggy and drizzling. She looked down at the plate in her hand and felt sick. Glancing back at the door behind her to be sure Sunshine wasn't watching, she dumped the plate's contents into the dumpster and then went back into the coffee shop.

Joe had left while she was gone; his cup of mocha was still full, and two large silver coins sat on the table beside it. She scooped up the coins and slipped them into the change pockets on her waitress smock. *These are really heavy*, she realized, feeling the way they made her smock sag. *What are they, Sacagawea dollars?*

She pulled a coin out and sat down at an empty table to scrutinize the round metal object more closely. It was a dull grey, but when Lupe rubbed one side with a cloth napkin, the highlights gleamed. *Tarnished silver, like old fine jewelry.* The coin was large, more than an inch wide. Although tarnished, it was not worn; the details were perfectly crisp and there were no scratches, as though it never been circulated. One side was embossed with an eagle and the words United States of America. In God We Trust. One Dollar. Lupe flipped the coin over. The other side bore an elegant woman's face, wearing a crown inscribed liberty. Beneath that, the date, 1896.

Díos mío. She wrapped the coin in a clean napkin and stuck it in her pocket. *Best way I can bag the evidence right now. This'll have to do till I get this to Ms. Kwan.* She yelled across the restaurant, "Sunshine, gotta run out for a minute. Emergency."

When she dashed out the shop's door, she found the fog had settled in grey coils through the street, like a vast chilly serpent. She could only see a few feet ahead in the cold darkness. She called out, "Joe! Hey, Joe! Where are you?" He couldn't have gone far.

Shivering, she turned down a pitch-black alley, then paused. *I'd be crazy to go in there alone. . . . But I'm onto something big.* Lupe remembered what the detective had told CSC about the thrill of finding a vital clue; was that what had driven her to enter this alley, despite the danger? Curiosity pushed her forward. Then, she could feel warmth radiating through the cold air: a sewer vent. She jumped when her foot suddenly pressed against cloth and flesh.

"J–Joe?"

A scratchy voice answered her. "Well, sounds like the little waitress. What're you doing here?"

She was shaking, but she said, "Joe, I need to know something. Those coins you left, where'd you get them?"

She could hear his breath wheeze in and out slowly.

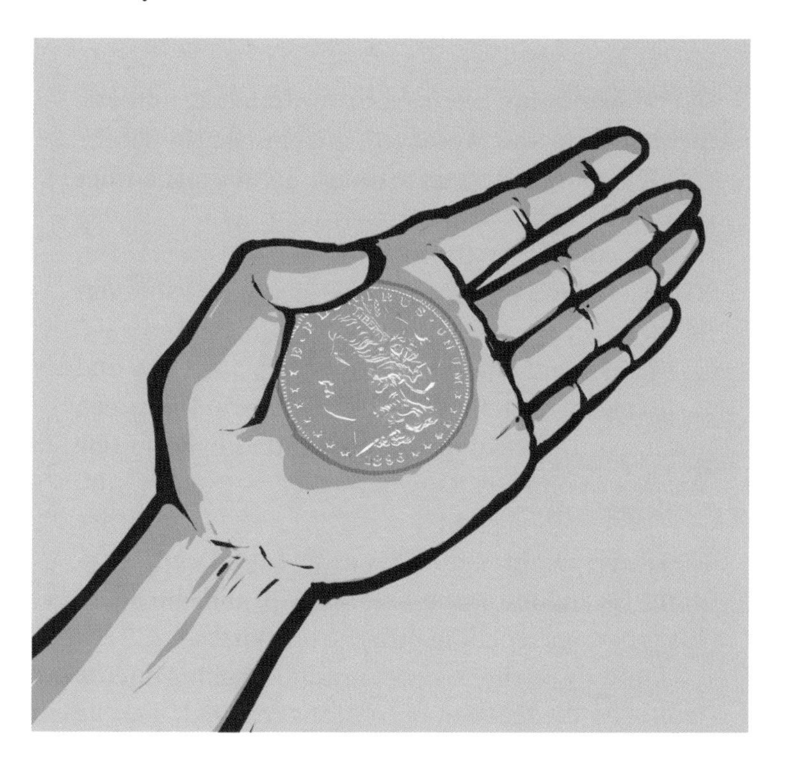

"This is really important," she added. "Where'd you get those coins?"

"None of your business. Go away."

Lupe squared her shoulders. "I'm not leaving till you tell me."

His reply finally came, a soft disembodied voice in the fog that made her skin crawl with goose bumps: "Found them in the wilderness."

"Where?"

"In the arroyo, just lyin' there."

"Just lying there, in the sand?"

"Yep."

Give me courage, Lupe prayed silently. "You're lying."

"How would you know?"

"Those coins were fresh, untouched. They've been hidden and preserved, not lying in the sand."

Her heart jolted as a rough hand grasped her wrist in vise-like grip and twisted it. "Ow!"

He pulled her down onto the wet pavement. Lupe choked, smelling his fetid breath. She was alone in utter darkness with a madman.

"Díos, ayudame," she whimpered.

"Now . . . listen . . . girl." He wheezed between each word. "Leave me alone. I didn't hurt no one for those coins."

"Who said you did?"

His grip tightened. "Stay away from Devil's Canyon!" He suddenly released his grip, and she heard his footsteps receding into the blackness.

Lupe lay on the cold wet ground, shaking uncontrollably. She had wet herself, she realized.

Chapter 4
STRANGERS IN THE CANYON

The next day, at lunchtime, Lupe noticed Ken Benally sitting alone at a picnic bench in the courtyard.

"Hey Ken."

"Hi Lupe."

"Where's Jessa?"

"She does yoga on Thursdays."

"You don't do yoga with her?"

"Nah, that's a chick thing." He pointed to the empty space next to him. "Join me?"

"Thanks."

"You don't have any lunch. Can I buy you a meal?"

"No thanks. Listen, Ken, I've stumbled onto something." Lupe told him about the coins and her frightening encounter with Joe the night before.

"Wow." Ken seemed genuinely impressed. He thought for a moment, then asked, "Did you get the e-mail Ms. Kwan sent to CSC today?"

"No."

He pulled a folded paper from his backpack and handed it to her.

```
LATEST DEVELOPMENTS
Ran analysis on evidence gathered
at Peshlaki's place. Determined
from spatter marks that someone
shot the dog from direction of
the arroyo. Fibers found on the
cactus are wool and synthetic
fiber, dyed blue, likely from an
expensive man's suit coat. Unable
to find anything on the note,
other than faint impressions of
two letters "u" and "r."
```

Lupe handed the paper back to Ken. He seemed lost in thought for a moment, then said, "Lupe, I think you and I should go back to the canyon after school and look around."

"Uh . . . okay." She wondered what Jessa would think about this. "Should I tell Mr. Chesterton?"

"Nah, sometimes two can find something better than a whole bunch of people tramping all over stuff."

"But we'll be alone out there. What if something happens?" Lupe remembered all too well the grip of Joe's fingers on her wrist the night before.

"I noticed Peshlaki has cell-phone service out there. I have my dad on speed dial, in case we need backup. We'll be fine." He smiled at her. "I'll pick you up in the south parking lot after school."

Later that afternoon, the two of them walked along a narrow path that cut through weeds and manzanilla bushes along the side of the arroyo. To their left and right, sandstone walls rose against the sky. Beyond the canyon's edge, they could hear the faint booming of thunder, and a moist breeze warned of rain. Overhead, however, the sky was brilliant blue. Lupe loved the quirks of Southwestern weather.

She glanced at the young man beside her; all afternoon she had asked herself, *Does he want me along on this trip because he thinks I'm smartest and most likely to find clues—or does he want to be alone with me because. . . ?*

Ken carried a digital camera. "It's not as good as the one Ms. Kwan uses for CSC, but it'll do," he explained. He had also brought a detailed trail map of Devil's Canyon, which he handed to Lupe. "Your job to navigate."

They came to a point where the trail narrowed to less than a foot, and Lupe's hiking boot dislodged a small avalanche of stones.

"Oooh!" she slid on her bottom into the arroyo.

"Whoops. You okay down there?"

Ken jumped down into the dry riverbed and offered a hand to pull her up. She reached out to him; he gave her hand a tug and then kept his fingers curled around hers. Suddenly, they were just inches apart, and she could feel his warm breath on her cheek. Their eyes met. She felt his other hand on her back, drawing her closer to him. . . .

And then the whining roar of an engine intruded into the canyon's stillness. They whirled around to see a four-wheeler skid to an abrupt sidewise stop beside them.

The driver was a middle-aged man, wearing a white Stetson, long-sleeved button-up shirt, and bolo tie. Lupe's heart jumped as she recognized the old medicine man's description of the stranger he had seen.

The man turned off the engine of his vehicle and glared at them. "What are you kids doing out here?"

"Taking a hike. We fell from the trail into the arroyo," Lupe replied.

"Looks to me like you were making out. Your parents know about this?"

"Hey, wait a minute," Ken interjected. "What are you doing out here?"

"None of your business, kid. This is public land."

"Yeah, but. . ." Lupe squeezed Ken's arm, and waited for him to follow her gaze. On the man's hip was a nickel-plated revolver.

"I see you're packing a sidearm," Ken said quietly.

"Perfectly legal." The man grinned. "Never know what you might have to shoot out here." He patted the pistol grip.

"Well, nice meeting you, Mr, uh . . . what did you say your name was?" Lupe was tugging at Ken's sleeve, trying to get away.

The stranger just looked at her, his hand on his gun.

The two teens backed away, then turned and scrambled up to the path. Lupe felt sweat dripping down her arms; she imagined the blast of a gun, the impact of a bullet tearing through her back. . . .

But that didn't happen. The man started up his quad and zoomed away the way he had come, leaving a trail of dust.

"Well," Ken mused, "that guy certainly seems capable of crime. Now we have two suspects."

Lupe was imagining how differently the afternoon could have ended: the stranger firing two shots, then dragging their bodies to some remote location, where he would cover them with brush. There was no way to tell if the stranger with the hat was just bad-tempered—or a psycho killer. For all Lupe knew, she was alive only because of a chance decision—like the random flip of a coin—that caused the man not shoot them. She shivered, despite the warm sunshine on her head.

The following day, Maeve walked up to Lupe at the end of study hall.

"Hey there, Stick Girl."

"Feel free to call me Lupe, Vampire Girl."

"Whatever. What do you think of this case?"

"It's getting strange . . . creepy."

"Yeah, I heard about your run-in with crazy Joe and the dude on the quad." Maeve gave an evil grin. "You rock, girl."

"Thanks. I guess."

A boy walked by and Maeve slapped his backside. "Freak!" he yelped. Maeve chuckled and turned back to Lupe, "By the way, I was surfing on my computer last night, and found something interesting about the company that sponsors us, Safe West Security, and that hot guy, Mr. McGinnis—"

"You dirty sneak!" Jessa thrust her red face between the two other girls. "You took off with my man, the two of you alone in the canyon."

Lupe sucked in a breath. "Jessa, I can explain. . . ."

"I don't need any explanation. When I called Ken, his dad said he was hiking in Devil's Canyon, and Katie Smith saw the two of you in Ken's truck after school—"

"Calm down! Nothing happened between me and your boyfriend!"

Maeve jumped into the discussion and said, "Well, Jessa, you shouldn't be surprised. If I were Ken, I'd want to be around a girl like Lupe, someone with, well, she's awful skinny, but she does have . . . *brains*." She emphasized the last word with a smirk.

"Shut up, Maeve," Lupe snapped. "You're not helping. Okay, Jessa, cool down. I was with Ken yesterday, that part is true. And we did go to Devil's Canyon. But it was all about the case. We were looking for more clues because I found these old coins and—"

"Did you touch him?" Jessa shouted.

"We were looking for—"

"Answer me."

"Jessa, nothing happened, just—"

"Just *what?*"

Lupe recalled the way she'd felt when she and Ken were in the bottom of the arroyo, their bodies pressed together; she felt her face flush.

"You were gettin' it on with my guy, weren't you?"

Lupe's tongue seemed paralyzed.

Jessa slapped Lupe's face.

Lupe put a hand on her stinging cheek. Voices echoed inside her head, *Eat your food . . . can't buy the TV . . . have to move . . . stay away from Devil's Canyon . . . dirty sneak!* Something inside her exploded. She jumped onto Jessa, grabbed a yellow dreadlock, and pulled.

Jessa shrieked, and the two went down onto the floor, yelling, pulling, and scratching.

Maeve jumped on a table and yelled, "Fight! Whee-hee!" She clapped and shook her hips like a cheerleader. A moment later, one of the combatants kicked a leg of the table, and Maeve lost her balance, falling hard onto the floor. She sent a swift kick into the fray with her hard-toed boot. Screams filled the cafeteria.

Eventually, the cafeteria monitors pulled them apart and dragged the girls, still yelling and thrashing, to the office.

None of the three girls had been involved in serious problems before, so the girls got off with little more than a warning. After school, Lupe slunk to room B1 and peeked cautiously in the door. The others had already arrived. As soon as Lupe sat down, the police department liaison began an obviously prepared speech.

"I understand that our young women—*all* of our young women—were involved in a fight. I don't have to tell you how disappointed we are." The three avoided her gaze. Ken Benally stared intently at a large poster on the wall, titled Periodic Table of the Elements.

Mr. Chesterton added, "The principal called me in during lunchtime." He sighed. "He explained in no uncertain terms that if there are any more incidents like today, this club is history."

Mr. McGinnis looked as if he were having a hard time suppressing a smile as he stood in the front of the room, looking at the ceiling and shaking his head. *Bet he had the girls fighting over him when he was in high school*, Lupe thought through her embarrassment. *Maybe he still does.*

"Before we do anything else," Ms. Kwan continued, "I need to know that you kids can get along. It's time to bury the hatchet, girls. Who would like to start?"

Maeve put her hand up. "That was a great fight. Haven't had so much fun in a long time. I want to thank Lupe and Jessa for spicing up a boring day. No hard feelings."

Ms. Kwan cleared her throat. "That wasn't exactly what I had in mind."

Lupe slid a hand into the air.

"Yes?"

"I lost control of myself." She stared down at her notebook. "Having problems lately. Sorry, it won't happen again."

The detective nodded approval, then turned toward the front row. "Jessa, something you'd like to add?"

"Yeah, Ms. Kwan, you are right-on about how we gotta get along in this club. Fighting is totally not what it's about. But you know how when someone does ya wrong you can't just sit there, right? So if anyone in the future tries to mess with my man, they better watch out."

Lupe put her head on the table. Ken looked as if he were memorizing the entire wall chart.

"All right," Mr. Chesterton said, "I'm going to assume there won't be any more problems like this. Next time, go for a punching bag instead of your classmates, okay? Now let's get back to the case. There are some interesting developments, aren't there, Ms. Kwan?"

"Yes," the detective agreed. "We interviewed our possible suspects. Joe Lester told us the same story he told Lupe, about finding the coins on the ground. It's not a crime leaving antique coins for a tip, so he's free to go. As to the stranger in the canyon, he says his name is Arnold Huston, and he's a freelance writer doing a series on the history of the Atchison, Topeka and Santa Fe Railroad. The man hasn't been formally accused of any crime, so we let him go also. I'm afraid we can't do anything more without tangible evidence and court orders."

"But," Mr. Chesterton prompted, "there is a new, more sinister development in this case."

"I'm afraid so," the police woman agreed. "Shortly after one this afternoon, a 9-1-1 call came in from a cell phone in Devil's Canyon, about a mile east of Mr. Peshlaki's place. The caller, a Mr. Norbert Feesham, is a tourist on vacation from Chicago.

He was hiking along the canyon taking pictures of the scenery, when someone shot at him. He was wounded in the shoulder, fortunately not in a life-threatening way."

Lupe, Ken, and Jessa gasped. Wire looked up from his computer screen, blinked. Maeve said, "Whoa!"

"Did the responding unit find any evidence of the shooter?" Ken asked.

"With the victim's cooperation, we were able to get some clues," Ms. Kwan explained. "Thankfully, he wasn't hurt much—just scared. Bandage, antiseptic, and some Gator-Aid, and he was able to cooperate with our crime scene team. Mr. Feesham told us he felt the bullet graze his arm before he heard the sound of the shot."

"So the shot came from a considerable distance away."

"That's right. To trace the shot, we asked him to stand in the exact spot where the bullet nicked him. We used his footprints to get the angle just right. With Feesham standing in his own tracks, one of our investigators used a tripod-mounted laser to trace the bullet's trajectory."

"And?"

"We walked along the beam, until it intersected a pile of fallen timber in the bottom of the arroyo. In the dirt there, we found a rough shoe-print. We took an impression, but it was too poor to determine much more than dimensions—a man's size 11 or 12. Nearby, we found something else: tracks from an ATV."

Ken and Lupe exchanged glances.

"We carefully noted the GPS coordinates of both the victim and the shooter in this incident, so we might be able to use our geographic profiling software if there are more crimes related to this case—and I fear there may be."

"What about the bullet? Did you go the other direction and look for that?" Wire asked.

"We did. It went upward into the canyon wall. We found the point of impact where it ricocheted, but despite several hours searching, no luck on the slug itself."

Lupe asked, "Do we know where our suspects were at the time?"

"No one has seen Joe Lester today, so we consider him a possible suspect, at least for now. We located Huston, half an hour after the shooting, two miles east in the arroyo on his ATV. He said he'd been taking notes for his article all afternoon, and had no one to vouch for him. So he could have done it, too. We took impressions of the tracks from his ATV, and they do match the tracks at the shooting site. His shoes are the right size, but that's not an uncommon dimension for an adult male. None of that establishes him as the shooter . . . but he is definitely a person of interest in this case."

"Sounds awful suspicious, if you ask me," Ken Benally whispered.

Wire put his hand up.

"Yes, Wire?"

"Did anyone think to ask where Mr. Peshlaki was at the time of the shooting?"

"Why?" Jessa asked. "He isn't a suspect."

"But," Lupe was thinking fast, "he does own a rifle with scope and ammo."

"We all like Mr. Peshlaki," Jessa insisted.

"But you have to use unsentimental logic if you want to solve crimes," Wire argued, "and the unlikeliest person may be our criminal. We didn't actually see the dog, and he could have made up his own threatening letter."

"Excellent!" Ms. Kwan affirmed. "Wire and Lupe are thinking like real detectives." Jessa stuck her tongue out at Lupe. The detective frowned at her and continued, "Trust no one. That same thought about Peshlaki occurred to us, also. Half an hour ago, our ranger found him a ridge near his Hogan with his rifle, loaded, in his lap. Said he was hunting rabbits for stew. So," Ms. Kwan concluded, "we have three possible suspects, none of them have alibis, but none of them can be linked to the shooting either." The detective lowered her voice. "Since longer range means less accuracy, we have to assume that the shooter didn't intend just to scratch Mr. Feesham. Someone was shooting to kill."

Lupe shuddered, thinking that twice now she had been near someone who could be a cold-blooded murderer. Her detective heroes in television mysteries and crime novels never seemed frightened—but when she looked at her arm, it was covered with goose bumps.

When Lupe arrived home that afternoon, her parents were waiting for her. Lupe's heart sank, knowing that the school must have called them about her fight with Jessa.

Her mother shook her head. "*Ay, Mija*, whatever were you thinking?"

"Mom, Dad, I'm *really* sorry. I won't do anything like this again."

"Darn right you won't," her mom agreed. "And to make sure, you're grounded on Saturdays when you're not working at the coffee shop. You can stay home and help your dad in the garage."

Lupe nodded.

"And if you're going to be helping me, may as well start now." Her dad pointed toward the door.

As she followed her father into the garage, he gestured toward a large red car. "This is Jaime Pasquale's ride. It's a beauty, but he wants it to look even better. First, we'll spray it all gold, then I'll air-brush some mural designs on it. Right now, this car is worth maybe ten grand. After I do some magic, twice that."

He pointed toward a large tank, standing upright like an oversized water heater. "Your job is to keep an eye on this compressed air tank and make sure the needle on the gauge stays between the yellow and red markings." He handed her a painter's face mask.

As her father sprayed metallic flake gold onto the surface of the classic car, Lupe's eyes roved back and forth between her dad's air gun, the car that was slowly turning color, and the gauge on the air tank.

Boy, this takes a long time. She began to feel faint and thought back to what she had eaten that day. Breakfast: one bite of toast, a quarter cup of coffee.

Lunch: nothing—she spent her lunch hour in the principal's office. Supper: nothing yet, the evening meal had been delayed because her parents were bawling her out. But she didn't feel hungry, and she didn't want to get fat, so this would be good for her.

Time dragged on. The hose hissed, the needle held steady. Then the room began to spin, slowly,

and the car and her dad went in and out of focus. She felt light-headed; the room was disappearing. She reached for the tank to steady herself.

Ka-boom! A sound like thunder brought her back to consciousness. She was sprawled across the huge compressed air tank, which she had apparently pushed over. The attachments atop the tank were gone, along with portions of the classic car, and most of the side of the garage. It looked as if a tornado had blown through the room. Broken glass was everywhere.

Father and daughter stared at one another.

"*Ay Díos*, Dad, I am so sorry!"

"We could have been killed." Raul Arellano leaned back against the hood of the smashed-up car, then glanced at the badly damaged vehicle. He groaned. "I let my insurance lapse to save money."

"You mean, we have to pay for—"

"Ten grand." Her father looked sick. "That car is totaled. Where am I supposed to come up with that?"

Lupe buried her face in her hands.

"Lupe, why? What happened?"

"I–I'm not sure. Maybe, because I didn't eat today. . ."

"You never eat. That's why you're just skin and bones."

"Dad, I'm sorry, I—"

"Sorry? That's all you can say, 'Sorry'? That won't pay ten thousand dollars. I have a job offer from Kustom Karations back where we used to live. I was going to say no, but now," he sighed, "there's no other way I can pay for all this damage. I'll call Karations and accept their offer. We'll put this house up for sale and move soon as we can." He pulled off his work gloves, threw them on the ground, and stomped into the house.

Lupe turned to the wall, where a glossy color picture of the Virgin of Guadalupe adorned a calendar. *Holy Mary, Mother of God, pray for us sinners.* . . . She recited silently and then thought, *My family is going to move now, I'm making a mess out of the club. . . . I'm worse than a sinner. I'm a total loser.*

Chapter 5
MAPPING MURDER

Lupe called in sick on Saturday for her work at Café Paradiso, and spent that day and the next in her bedroom. Come Monday, she decided to drag herself into school, if only to get away from home.

At the conclusion of biology class, Mr. Chesterton pulled her aside and asked, "Do you have a theory about who threatened Peshlaki and shot at Feesham?"

"I'd say Arnold Huston, the man on the ATV."

"Think so? Why?"

"He appeared just before trouble began, has a good way to get around the canyon, he's armed, and he's being evasive when questioned. So I think that makes him a likely suspect."

Mr. Chesterton's lips twisted. "I don't think so."

"Why not?"

"Because," the science teacher replied, "I got this e-mail from Ms. Kwan just a few minutes ago." He handed Lupe a printout, and her breath caught as she read the words.

```
MURDER VICTIM
Our former suspect, Arnold
Huston, was found dead in
Devil's Canyon early this
morning, shot in the back.
More details this afternoon
at CSC meeting.
```

After school, the students gathered for club before Ms. Kwan and Mr. McGinnis arrived. There were some catty glances between Jessa and Lupe, but speculation about the murder dominated the discussion among the teens.

The detective came with her laptop, which Mr. Chesterton patched into the classroom overhead projector. "Doubtless you've heard by now," the detective began, "that our case has turned into a murder. This morning at 7 am, a volunteer with the Coconino County Conservation program was tracking elk at the Flagstaff end of Devil's Canyon. He was following a large bull along the bottom of the arroyo, when he came upon a man's body. It was wearing a white shirt, lying face down in the dry riverbed. There was an ATV parked a few yards from the corpse, and a white hat caught in a bush about fifty feet away. I arrived with two other detectives an hour later. Our photographer carefully recorded the scene, and we also analyzed the area with a total geographic profiling system."

"Have you made a positive ID on the body?" Wire asked.

"His driver's license and credit cards were in his wallet. The image on his license matched his appearance. We still have to find kin or close acquaintance to be one-hundred-percent certain, but I'm willing to bet it's Huston. Okay, students, brace yourselves. The next image may upset you." Ms. Kwan touched a button on the remote, and a life-sized image of the dead man, lying as he was found at the scene, appeared on the screen.

Lupe gasped.

Maeve picked at a black fingernail and remarked, "That dark spot—entrance hole for the bullet?"

"It is. The coroner's initial autopsy says a single bullet went into his back, just missing the spinal cord and nicking a vertebra, then passed through the victim's right ventricle, and shattered his sternum on the way out. There are no powder marks on the dead man's shirt, so the shooter was some distance away."

"The murderer is a good marksman." Ken's voice was grim. "That was a difficult shot."

"We thought the same. He must have practiced gunning for a human heart."

"Huston's revolver is in his holster, I see."

"That's right."

"Was it fired?"

"Eight bullets in eight chambers."

"He didn't see his assailant, then."

"Never knew he was being stalked," Ms. Kwan agreed. "This is going to get a bit more grisly now. Are you sure can you stomach it?" Without waiting for a reply, she pressed the remote again, and the image changed to the body lying on a gurney, seen from the top. A huge hole opened through the man's chest, accompanied by a copious amount of blood. Jessa gagged into her hand.

"The bullet went right through." Maeve leaned forward, obviously fascinated.

Ms. Kwan nodded. "A powerful firearm did this. Exit wounds aren't always so gory—sometimes the bullet goes out as cleanly as it goes in—but this one was dragging a lot of flesh and bone along with it."

"Did you find the slug?" Ken asked.

"We did. It only went another fifteen feet."

Another picture, this time of a misshapen piece of metal.

"Can you ID that?" Wire inquired.

".45 caliber. It's pretty banged up, going through all that skin and bone, and then hitting a rock."

"Were you able to establish trajectory for the bullet?"

"We were. We measured the height from the soles of Huston's shoes to the bullet hole, calculated the angle and direction of the shot, and traced back along a laser beam. We didn't find any evidence of the shooter's location, though. The shot was horizontal with the ground, so it could have come from almost any point."

"What was time of death?" Lupe asked.

"The coroner's report says he died about two hours before we arrived. His body temp had only gone down three degrees, and had not begun to stiffen at all," Ms. Kwan replied. "A body loses heat at approximately a degree and a half per hour.

That's not an exact measure, but we're guessing he was shot around nine am."

"Was the body moved after the killing?"

"Far as we can tell, the body was untouched. Blood spatter on the ground just in front of the body is what we'd expect if he was shot from the back and then fell forwards. Likewise, the ATV seems to be where he parked it. Looks like his hat blew off at the moment of impact and wind carried it into the bush. The MO appears to be that of a sniper—the perpetrator simply shot him in the back, from a distance, and then walked away. Huston's wallet was still in his pocket, gun at his side, everything in place."

"Fingerprints, shoeprints, tire tracks?" asked Wire. "Any sign of the shooter at the site?"

"We found tire tracks fifty yards north of the body, in the arroyo. The tracks were from a jeep or similar off-road vehicle. We took photos and casts, then ID'd the brand and size of tire back at the lab. It's common in this area: at least a hundred people in Coconino County have vehicles using that tire type. We have an officer calling shops to compile a list of everyone who has bought similar tires over the past four years. We'll run background checks on all those names, but frankly, we're not very hopeful." The detective paused, then added, "We didn't find any hairs, fibers or footprints. Whoever did this knows how to cover up evidence. Also, it was windy out there this morning, and that would remove most tracks in the loose sand."

"Anything of interest among the victim's belongings on the ATV?" Ken asked.

"Just a spare gas tank and maps of the canyon."

"Wait a minute," cried Lupe. "Didn't Huston tell the ranger last week that he was writing notes?"

"He did," Ms. Kwan agreed.

"So where's his notebook?"

The detective smiled, gave Lupe a thumbs-up sign. "Let's check on that." She typed a reminder into her laptop.

"So . . . that's all we have for now?" Mr. Chesterton queried.

"Oh, no. This was just the start," Ms. Kwan replied. "We've been busy today."

Lupe had been trying not to react the way Jessa had to the gory image of the dead man, but she realized now that the few bites of veggie sandwich and yogurt from her lunch were trying to come back up, pushing through her esophagus in a most unpleasant, burning manner. Her mind flashed back and forth between the very alive man who had accosted her just last week and the corpse in the pictures. She choked her food down again.

Ms. Kwan was saying, "The frustration of this Devil's Canyon case is that we don't have much to go on. We have no witness to any of the crimes, and little in the way of physical evidence. What we've found—a few fibers of cloth, a rough footprint, tire tracks—might help to build a case if we had the perpetrator, but these clues aren't enough to locate the shooter. So we've applied the process of geographic profiling."

Mr. McGinnis had been sitting quietly on a stool, paying careful attention to the proceedings. Now the well-dressed club sponsor reminded the students, "Using equipment that was partially sponsored by Safe West Security."

Not the time for a commercial, Lupe thought. *He may be cute, but he's a jerk.*

Ms. Kwan continued as though Mr. McGinnis hadn't spoken. "This situation isn't ideal for geographical profiling—it works best if at least five related crimes enter into the equation. We have just three: Peshlaki's dog, the shot at Mr. Feesham, and Mr. Huston's murder."

"Great!" Maeve whispered. "Now all we have to do is wait for two more bodies to show up."

"You are one sick puppy," Lupe whispered back.

The detective clicked on her remote again, and a three-dimensional map appeared on the screen. "I spent the last few hours using our new software system, called Predator, to come at this case from a geographic perspective. As I told you earlier, the Southwestern wilderness is famous for close relationships between people and places, so that suggests this approach may be fruitful, despite the low number of related incidents. What you see is a large section of Devil's Canyon, with the location of all three crimes. We established the position of all three crimes using GPS."

Jessa stared into space with a glazed expression, but Wire was hanging on the detective's every word.

Nancy Drew never did this kind of stuff, Lupe reflected.

Ms. Kwan explained the map on the projection screen. "Crime scenes are displayed on the map in order of occurrence. In the middle, the number 1 is Peshlaki's place, where someone shot his dog.

Following the canyon floor to the northeast of that, just before we enter Reservation land, is where Feesham was wounded, with the number 2. And down to the southwest from Peshlaki's place, following the arroyo, is where Huston was killed, number 3 on the map."

"Why is that line between 2 and 3 brighter on the screen?" Jessa asked.

"That's called the jeopardy surface, the area where our criminal is most likely to strike again."

"Looks awful big," Maeve observed.

"Afraid so," the detective agreed. "From the place where Feesham was wounded to the point where Huston was murdered is twenty miles. In between, there are hundreds of boulders, rockslides, hoodoos, juniper, and piñon trees—a virtual maze."

"My ancestors are Apache and Navajo," Ken Benally said. "And they managed to hide from whole regiments of cavalry in that very same canyon."

"So," Jessa asked, "what's next?"

"We'll keep several teams patrolling the area. Unfortunately, we have a pattern of escalating behavior, a vast area with numerous hiding spots, few leads, and a killer who needs to be arrested soon or he's likely to murder again."

An hour later, Lupe dragged her feet along the path to home. She was feeling tired and dizzy, and she was dreading facing her parents. When her cell phone buzzed, she welcomed the distraction. A text message read:

`Meet tonight 9PM Paradiso. Tell no one. Wire.`

What's up? she wondered and then gathered her courage to go inside her house.

She arrived at the café a few minutes before nine, and found Wire and Maeve at a table in the back of the shop. She noticed Maeve had two empty coffee cups beside her. Both were staring at Wire's laptop.

"Wait till you see what we've got!" Maeve exclaimed. "This is more fun than any man."

"Is that all you ever think about? Men?"

"Nah, I think about death more than I do men." The dark-clad girl glanced toward the doorway. "Oh, good. Here come the kewpie dolls."

Ken and Jessa were en route toward the back table, Jessa with her arm twined firmly around the Native boy's waist. She smirked at Lupe.

"What's up?" Ken asked.

"Better sit down," Wire replied. "This may take a while."

He punched a button and turned the laptop toward the others, revealing an image similar to Ms. Kwan's 3-D map of the canyon, with the numbered crime scenes.

"How'd you do that?" Jessa asked.

"Found satellite views of the canyon, then ran those through a topographical mapping program."

"Not bad."

"This afternoon's CSC meeting was very informative," Wire continued. "I hadn't thought of the geographic approach to this case. The PD hasn't made much headway yet with their Predator program, but they've started down the right track."

"Think you can do better?" Ken gave Wire a doubtful look.

"Of course. They don't spend enough time doing RPGs."

"What?"

"Online role playing games—RPGs. They teach you to think fast, see space three-dimensionally, and compete with live human beings. They're a perfect simulation for a situation like this case." Wire tapped his forehead. "And I have the perfect brain for matching up the evidence with the computer programs. The police are looking at crimes and victims—but that's not the real goal of the game. The real goal is—"

"The treasure!" Lupe exclaimed.

"Exactly. Threats and shootings are just the aftermath of greed. Like Ms. Kwan says, you have to understand the land—and Northern Arizona is soaked with blood shed over centuries of lusting after precious metals. Find the treasure site and I guarantee you, we will find the shooter and solve these crimes as well."

"But we don't know where the treasure is."

Wire and Maeve smiled mysteriously.

"First step," Wire said, "is to begin with what we do know about that treasure."

"The robbers went east. Their horses' prints disappeared into the arroyo," Lupe recalled. "Felicity H. said the robbers were in a hurry to be on their way, as they had to reach a cave by sundown."

The thin boy nodded. "I found a Web site, Great Robberies of the Old West. It has a map marked with the train holdup location. So I superimposed that onto our crime scene map." He touched a key, and a big red arrow appeared between numbers 3 and 1 on the screen. "That's our starting point."

"Okay, but how can you tell where they wound up from there? Ms. Kwan says that canyon is like a maze."

"Patience, all shall be revealed. The next step is to figure how far the robbers went. Based on their remarks, we know they had just time to reach their destination before dark. This was mid-March, and sundown was 5:45 pm. The hold-up took place at 2:10 in the afternoon, so they had three and a half hours of travel time to the cave where they stashed the loot."

"How fast were they going?" Lupe wondered.

Wire nodded. "You're asking the right question."

"They would have started out trotting," Jessa put in—apparently she knew something about horses—"but not for long. The horses were weighed down with silver dollars and gold bars. They probably slowed to a walk soon as they rounded the bend."

"So you *do* have some grey matter between those dreadlocks," Maeve said. "That's what Wire and I came up with also."

"So," Wire continued, "we figured four miles per hour as their speed."

"They went fourteen miles up the canyon. Map that and you're near the treasure site," Lupe thought aloud.

Wire poked at the keyboard, and a large red circle appeared on the topographical view of the canyon.

“That’s part of Ms. Kwan’s jeopardy surface,” Ken said. “Just north of Peshlaki’s place. You’ve narrowed things down, but with all the rough terrain out there, it could still take months to find the cave.”

“Not done yet.” Wire pressed a few more keys, and the view zoomed into the treasure’s zone circle; from the canyon floor, four side-canyons extended outward, like spokes of a big wheel.

“How do you know whether the robbers went down one of those side-canyons?” Lupe asked.

“Enter another factor—water,” Wire replied. “I don’t think the train robbers wanted their treasure flooded out. I checked the National Weather Service Web site. The canyon can get up to thirty inches of water in a single downpour. So, assuming the thieves would know that, I calculated this topography program to take thirty inches off the bottom, and—look at this.” He typed into the laptop again, and the view changed. Only two of the side-canyons remained.

“The treasure is in one of those two off-shoots from the canyon.” Lupe was so excited she forgot her other troubles. “With several weeks of searching, someone should be able to find it.”

“Yes, but there’s one final step. What do we need in these side-canyons if we want to hide a treasure?”

“A cave?”

“Right. And it’s an uncharted cave, or the treasure would have been found before now. So what do we know about caves in this part of the world?” He looked around at the group.

"Well, there's a lava cave where I've been to some wild parties," Jessa said. "But it's nowhere near Devil's Canyon."

"But lava caves are formed in what?"

"Volcanic rock."

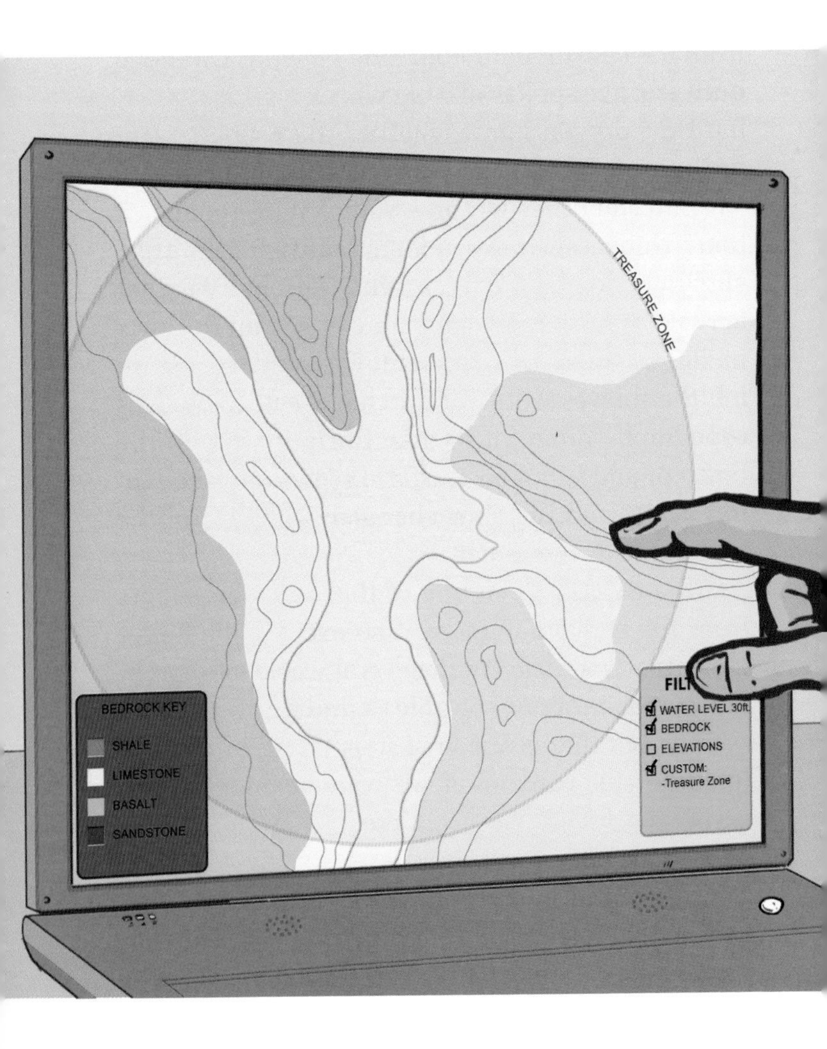

"Basalt, to be exact. I found a state geological survey map of Devil's Canyon, taken back in the 1950s and just recently posted online." He punched at the keyboard yet again. "And—voila! The tip of that canyon going off to the east is formed of basalt. That's where we'll fine a cave. And that's where the treasure is."

"Wait a minute," Jessa protested. "People have been looking for that treasure for years. My grandfather looked all over Devil's Canyon, spent months in the wilderness with his burro and pickaxe. I'm sure Peshlaki and a lot of other folks have looked, too. You think you can sit here in one afternoon and find that treasure on your laptop, without even leaving this coffee shop?"

"Only one way to find out," Wire replied. "I'll bet a hundred bucks the treasure is here." He pointed at the highlighted spot on the computer map.

"Wow." Lupe was genuinely impressed. "Let's get on the phone and call Mr. Chesterton, right now."

Wire and Maeve frowned at her.

"Oh, no . . . you're not thinking. . . ?"

"Finders keepers," Maeve whispered, her eyes gleaming. "Half a million dollars."

"But there's a murderer out there."

"Finders keepers," the girl in black hissed more loudly.

"This could be an epic adventure," Jessa said slowly. "It's the kind of thing I could spend the rest of my life writing and singing about—finding a real, hidden treasure."

"'The Ballad of Devil's Canyon,'" Maeve smirked.

"This is my way to make a mark on the computer world," Wire added. "You're all crazy—this is a job for the police department," Ken argued.

Lupe smiled at him. *One sane ally.*

"Ken baby." Jessa looked at him with big doe eyes. "You haven't been very nice to your girl lately. Don't you think you could do this just for me, to show me you still love me?" She pressed her body against his side.

Ken stared at the ground.

I'm gonna barf, Lupe thought.

Maeve's black-coated lips curled into a Cheshire cat grin. "Well, Lupe, you can stay home alone. The rest of us can find the treasure without you."

"But . . . how are you going to get there? You'll need some kind of transportation."

"My uncle lives just north of there, on the edge of the Rez," Ken said slowly. "I'm sure he'd lend us horses."

Jessa squeezed his arm.

"Tomorrow is a teachers' in-service day at school, so no classes," Wire added. "If we start out by eight, we can be at the treasure zone by noon. Lupe, are you with us or against us?"

She struggled to breathe. "I . . . I could tell on all of you."

"You could," Maeve agreed. "And I have a book of mediaeval tortures I've always wanted to try."

"We know where you live." Jessa's voice was heavy with threat.

"Forget that, Lupe," Wire put in. "No one is going to make you do anything you don't want to do. But do you really want to pass up this chance to become rich and famous?"

Lupe imagined giving her father a heavy bag full of silver and gold. *Here, Dad, this will pay for the damaged car—and we won't have to move.* She visualized the proud look on her father's face.

"I'll go with you, and I won't tell a soul," she said. "But on one condition."

The others waited.

"We only go into the canyon for the treasure—nothing else. There's a killer loose. We don't know if it's homeless Joe or Peshlaki or whoever. So anyone we meet in there could be the murderer."

The others nodded.

"Here's the deal. We see or hear anyone in the canyon—we turn around and get out of there fast as we can."

"Makes sense," Wire agreed. "I want to find the treasure, not take risks."

Maeve nodded. "Whatever."

"Okay," Jessa agreed.

"Good." Wire said. "We'll meet at the parking lot here at quarter to eight."

Lupe hoped she had made the right decision.

Chapter 6
DEAD-MAN'S BONES

"Wire, you sure we're still heading toward the treasure site?"

The five teens rode single file on a trail beside the arroyo, halfway up the canyon's side. Jessa led the group on a sorrel mare, followed by Lupe on a buckskin pony, and then Ken astride a chestnut gelding. These three were experienced equestrians, enjoying the chance to ride on horseback. Behind them, however, Maeve cursed and grimaced; she had struggled for hours to find a comfortable rhythm on a docile, chubby mare. Wire lagged behind the group, trying to read his pocket phone-computer and not fall off a strawberry roan.

"I've checked our GPS coordinates the whole way, comparing with the satellite map of the canyon. Next branch to our right is the treasure spot. Hey, no, horsey! This-way!" He pulled on the reigns as the roan tried to drift off the trail for a bite of tempting sweet grass.

Lupe chuckled.

"Makin' fun of me?" Wire asked.

"I'm not laughing with you, Wire—I'm laughing at you."

"Thanks. I'll remember that when we find the treasure."

Lupe laughed. The sun was warm on her head, and she was feeling more at peace than she had in days.

Suddenly, Jessa's mare gave a frightened neigh that sounded like a scream. The horse reared, twisted sideways, reared again.

"Whoa—whoa!" Jessa struggled to control her mount. But when the horse bucked yet again, Jessa flew sideways, her foot in the stirrup. Then her foot pulled out of her shoe, and Jessa rolled over the dusty rim of the canyon.

She landed in a pit several yards below the trail.

"Jessa!" Ken yelled, "You hurt?"

The only answer was a terrified scream as Jessa scrambled to her feet. "Snakes!"

Three writhing shapes made esses in the sand beside Jessa. Lupe stared in horror at their dark brown bodies patterned with lighter diamonds. Rattlers. Each as long as a man is tall.

One of them flew at the blond girl, fangs opened wide. It struck the thick heel of her boot, and then she crushed its head into a rock. The snake's body continued to writhe for several moments. The other two rattlers hissed but did not strike.

Lupe imagined how Jessa must feel, surrounded by hissing death. Before she could think any further, Lupe jumped off her horse and scrambled toward the pit.

"Lupe, no!" She barely heard Ken's voice above the sound of her pounding heart. She slid on her bottom, grabbed small ledges for handholds. Then the ground gave way. She skidded toward the snake pit.

At the last second, just above the pit's edge, Lupe grasped a bush.

"Grab onto my belt!" she shouted to Jessa. She held tight to the bush, heard the snakes' rattle. Then Jessa grabbed her waist and pulled herself upward.

"No!" Lupe screamed as the bush's roots pulled out of the soil.

In another moment, she knew they would both fall on the lethal reptiles.

"Got you!" Lupe felt hands under her armpits as she heard Ken's voice. She turned her head and saw that he, Maeve, and Wire had formed a human ladder on the rock wall leading to the trail. Jessa tightened her grasp around Lupe's waist as the other club members pulled the girls toward safety.

A few minutes later, they were back on the trail. The horses grazed peacefully on grass and bushes; their riders lay on the ground beside them, panting from exhaustion and fear.

"Lupe?" Jessa propped herself up on her elbows and looked at the other girl. "You saved my life."

Was that a thank you, Lupe wondered, *or just a statement of fact?*

"I—uh—I owe you."

Lupe wanted to say, So give me a chance with Ken Benally, but she held her tongue. She lay on her back, her eyes shut, catching her breath. "So what happened to your horse?" she asked finally. "Why did it rear like that?"

"It was a trap." Maeve pointed to a rope snare that lay now across the trail.

"Right above a rattler's lair," added Wire.

"Rattlers aren't social creatures," Ken pointed out. "You never see them in threes normally. Someone put those snakes in there."

Wire nodded. "Well, that proves my theory."

"Huh?"

"We're almost to the treasure. Somebody wants to scare people away."

Ken glanced at the girls, covered with dirt, scratches, and sweat. "You two want to go on?"

Lupe and Jessa exchanged glances, nodded.

Half an hour later, the five dismounted in a side-canyon. Ken shaded his eyes and squinted at the rock walls around them. "I don't see any cave."

"Can't believe I tortured my bottom this whole day for nothing," Maeve growled.

Jessa was staring at a large rock nestled against the edge of the ravine. "That is so ugly."

Maeve shook her head. "It's a rock, Jessa—not a work of art."

"But it ruins the whole effect of that rock face."

"You're an idiot. Rocks don't have to be pretty. They just exist."

Jessa walked over, put her hand on the giant stone. "Feels funny. Like paint."

Lupe walked over, scrutinized the boulder. "It's fake."

The teens exchanged glances, then put their shoulders to one side of the large, rounded object. It rolled easily, revealing a dark hole.

"I'll be darned!" Ken exclaimed.

"The treasure cave, no doubt." Wire gave a satisfied grin.

Ken pulled a small flashlight out of his pocket and walked through the hole in the canyon side; the others followed on his heels.

He moved the circle of yellowish light from the flashlight around the floor, examining the scene. The cave was thirty to forty feet deep. In the middle of it, empty rotted bags lay on the dirt. A handful of scattered coins littered the floor.

"Where's the treasure?"

"Someone took it."

"Oh, yuck!" Just beside the mouth of the cave was a skeleton, desiccated ribs and skull facing the ceiling. Next to it lay a rusted six-shooter

"Eesh!" Jessa made a gagging sound as the flashlight's beam illumined two more skeletons. One lay face down in the middle of the pile of bags; another sat crumpled along the side of the cavern, facing toward the entrance, finger bone still holding the trigger of another badly oxidized handgun.

The teens were silent for a minute, each grappling with the discovery. Then Jessa said, "Well, three skeletons—guess we know why the robbers disappeared from history. But . . . what happened to them?"

Maeve picked up the rusty revolver by the remains nearest the door. *How can she touch that moldy, dead-man's gun?* Lupe wondered.

"Be careful," Wire protested. "You shouldn't touch those—they may be a century old, but this is still a crime scene. Historians will want to study this place."

Maeve made a rude gesture and continued her examination. "Four bullets in the gun," she reported. "He got two shots off."

"A shot for each of those two, but what happened to him?"

Maeve gestured toward the skeleton that lay against the wall. "Ken, check that gun out?"

He shook his head. "My elders taught me never to touch dead people."

"Gimme that flashlight." Maeve picked up the other revolver, flicked the piece of bone out of the trigger guard, and flashed the light on it. "One bullet gone. Must've nailed the guy by the door."

"I would guess," Wire reasoned aloud, "that the doorkeeper here tried to do in his companions. Greedy fellow decided he'd keep the treasure for himself. But this one," he pointed toward the skeleton crumpled against the wall, "got a shot off in return, before dying. So, in the end, the treasure just belonged to three skeletons."

"Not anymore," Lupe corrected. "Now the treasure belongs to whoever placed that phony rock over the entrance and took the silver and gold from those bags."

"But who?"

"Answer that, and this whole mystery is solved."

As Lupe spoke, they heard the sound of an engine grinding in low gear, just outside the cave entrance.

Maeve turned off the flashlight and the teens huddled toward the back of the cavern. Footsteps crunched outside; then the silhouette of a man blocked the light of the entrance. In his hand was

the longest sidearm Lupe had ever seen. From the man's other hand, a flashlight beam probed into the darkness, revealing the five huddled young people. The revolver pointed directly toward them.

Maeve pointed her light at the figure in the entrance. Jessa let out a squeak of relief. "Mr. McGinnis! I'm so happy to see you."

"Turn that light off. It's in my eyes."

Maeve quickly complied.

Lupe noticed that McGinnis's hand cannon stayed leveled at them. "Jessa," she whispered, "I don't think he's here to help us." She recalled Mr. Chesterton's advice at their first meeting: *Expect the unexpected.*

"That's some howitzer you've got," Maeve said shakily.

McGinnis didn't respond; the gun still aimed in their direction.

"Buntline special," Wire whispered.

"Forty-five caliber," Ken added.

The man gave a grim chuckle. "Just like my great-grandpa used, and now it has a notch in the handle like his did."

"Your grandpa. . ." Lupe had a flash of insight. "Maeve, before Jessa and I got into our little tussle, you were going to tell me something."

"Yeah, Safe West Security, before a series of sales and mergers, used to be—"

Lupe already knew the answer. "Pinkerton Detective Agency, right?"

"Yep."

"And big Jake M, name withheld by the paper"—the pieces of the puzzle were snapping into place—"no doubt stood for Big Jake McGinnis. Quite the family tradition."

The man with the long revolver gave a sardonic smile.

"But," Jessa said feebly, "Big Jake was one of the good guys. He guarded the treasure."

"That's what he wanted everyone to think," Lupe replied. "I always knew there was something fishy about his story."

"Something fishy?"

"Yes, he was out cold when the bandits took off—least that's what he told the little girl bystander—but as soon as he stood up, he knew they'd gone east. How'd he know that if he was unconscious when they left?"

Ken whistled. "He was in with the robbers, just pretended to get knocked out."

McGuiness chuckled again. "Congratulations. When I saw you kids the first time, I thought you were a bunch of freaks. But I guess they picked real detectives after all." He pointed to the skeletal remains nearest the door. "Pinetree Bill there promised Jake a fifth of the treasure, providing he'd help with the heist. When they shot it out, great-grand pappy nailed the other two Pinkertons right by his side, before playin' possum. Then Bill's gang took off. They were supposed to deliver a map of the treasure, once it was hid. Map never came, though. The story's been handed down through four generations of McGinnisses, so we've been waitin' a while to get our share."

"But," Jessa asked, "why did you sponsor Crime Scene club?"

Lupe didn't wait for the man's answer. "Because what better way to keep an eye on police department activities and protect his own interests without raising suspicion?" She turned to McGinnis.

"Then you tried to scare Peshlaki away."

"Thanks to computer mapping, I pretty much figured out where the treasure had to be." The man looked smug.

They'd never thought, Lupe realized, that the bad guys in a case might use the same sort of technology as the good guys—and achieve similar results.

McGinnis was saying, "I guessed it was right in Peshlaki's backyard—but he was awful hard to sneak around."

"And you shot at Feesham, the tourist," Ken put in.

"Tourist? That's a joke," the man replied. "He was Huston's partner, and both of them are professional treasure hunters. Don't tell me you believed that crap about Feesham being a tourist and Huston researching a railroad book?" McGinnis looked thoughtful. The gun in his hand never wavered. "I was hoping Feesham would be the first notch on this baby." He patted the long barrel of his six-gun lovingly. "But the wind changed at the last moment, ruined my shot."

He enjoys killing. Shivers crawled up Lupe's spine.

"At least Feesham had sense to get out of Dodge, in a hurry," McGinnis continued. "Huston was more determined. He kept snooping. In fact, he found this place just a few days after I did. I'd already emptied out all the gold, but he got in here at the crack of dawn yesterday and took all kinds of notes. Had to follow him back toward Flagstaff and plug 'im twenty miles away from here, so as not to arouse more interest in this location."

He wants to boast about his crimes, Lupe realized. *And he thinks we're the only ones he'll ever get to tell.* "Huston's notebook?" she asked, deciding she'd oblige him. At least it kept him talking.

"Big hassle, whisking away footprints and tire tracks to get that off his four-wheeler."

"Now what?" Jessa's voice was quiet.

"I drive to an airfield on the Reservation, and then—party time. Can't wait to get my hands on those gorgeous Mexican women."

Yeah, thought Lupe, *they'll never know what a madman this particular rich gringo is.* She shifted her position, feeling suddenly panicked and dizzy.

"Sit still," McGinnis snapped. "If anyone tries to move—" He waved his pistol in their direction, then backed out of the cave.

The teens heard his steps, back and forth between the car and cave entrance.

"Do we try and rush out?" Maeve whispered.

"No way," Ken replied. "He'd shoot us all."

"So what do we do?"

"Wait."

"And pray," Lupe added.

And then an explosion like a cannon shot sent rocks and pebbles scattering.

Chapter 7
COURAGE

For an eerie couple of minutes, Lupe could hear nothing but a strange ringing noise in her ears. Then she began to discern voices, like faraway whispers.

"Everyone alive?"

"What?"

"Can't hear anything."

"Ooh, there's sticky stuff on my forehead. . . ."

"My knee hurts."

Maeve flicked on the flashlight, moved it slowly over the group. Lupe saw that several of the others had nasty-looking bruises and sores, but apparently no one was seriously injured. They were all covered with fine white dust, like South Sea Natives painted for some exotic funeral rite.

"What happened?" Jessa asked.

"He blasted the cave shut." Ken's voice was grim.

"Why didn't he just shoot us?"

"I don't like getting into that guy's brain, but I think he wanted us to die painfully, wounded by the explosion, or from starvation, or lack of air. . . ."

"I thought he was cute," Jessa said angrily. "He's inhuman!"

"Hey, speaking of inhuman," Maeve said in a creepy tone, "did you guys see that movie about those women who go down into the cave, and then one of them gets hurt, and there are these creatures that live down there. . . ."

"Knock it off!" Jessa pleaded.

"I think I just saw something moving." Maeve's voice sounding hollow, but Lupe thought she could hear the grin she was struggling to control.

"Shut up!"

"Oh all right. Wire, why'd you get us into this mess?" The dark-clad girl pointed her light at the boy who was trying to clean his spectacles, checking his pocket computer.

"You should talk, Maeve," Ken snapped. "This was your idiot notion as much as his."

"Ken, why did you go along with them?" Jessa whined.

"What?! If you hadn't put me up to it, I never—"

"Quiet, all of you!" Lupe shouted. "We all chose this. So let's think our way out of here just like we thought our way into this mess."

Silence.

"I'm sure the answer is no, but does anyone have cell service?"

No one did.

"Is it my imagination," Jessa asked in a small voice, "or is the air getting staler?"

"It's getting worse," Wire agreed. "We're using up oxygen fast."

Lupe was thinking hard. "Go back over the steps that got us here. We did computer mapping, then figured how far the bandits traveled from the train. . . ."

"Then looked for areas that wouldn't flood," Wire continued.

"Hey, wait a minute." Lupe felt a glimmering of an idea. "We picked this site because it was made of volcanic rock, right?"

"So?"

"From what I recall of geology class, volcanic rock usually has lots of tunnels and holes, like a great big honeycomb."

"That's right." Wire sounded thoughtful.

Maeve cast her light around the room. Fine particles of floating dust made the flashlight beam look almost as solid as the rock face. She swept the beam clear around, then backed it up to illumine a dark slit, like a cat's eye, about four feet above the floor on one side of the room.

There!

Ken stood up, wincing, and walked to the dark space. He stuck his hand in. "It's an opening all right. Awful thin, though."

"Well." Lupe was struggling to breathe. "One thing people keep telling me—though I don't believe it—is that I'm skinny. Wish I was thinner, but let's see if I'm skinny enough. . . ." She stretched her aching legs and pulled herself slowly up into the crevice. "Maeve, give me that light."

Lupe began to crawl through the tiny dark space. Dirt and dust scraped beneath her elbows and chin; the jagged lava rock surface above scratched her back. Tiny razor shards of rock on the rough walls tore little pieces off her clothes and skin. As she inched forward, the ceiling pressed down, squeezing her into a still smaller space. She could no longer proceed on her arms and legs, so she slid forward on her chest and pelvis, wriggling like a flattened worm through the ground. She heard Ken crawl in behind her and wondered how far he would get. He was thicker than she was, and there was barely room for her shoulders now. She tried not to think about the weight of all that rock pressing around her.

Her flashlight began to flicker. "Turning this off, gotta save batteries."

Behind her, Ken grunted approval.

Slowly, slowly, she inched through pitch blackness, unseen rock pressing tighter above and below. She was fighting for breath now, gasping for air in the constricted passage. Then—

Something tiny moved under her chin.

She shrieked, her voice muffled by the rock. Pain shot through her compressed chest.

"What?" Ken rasped behind her.

"S–sp–spider."

Her limbs spasmed, waves of terror rolled through her. The sides of the cave felt like they were pressing in, crushing her like a fly.

"Catch your breath, focus. Use the light if you need to." Ken's voice was calm, soothing.

This is what death must be like. Virgen de Guadalupe, ayudame. Help me!

"Lupe, talk to me."

She sucked in a deep breath. "Spider's gone. Pressing on."

She resumed the slow journey into darkness. And then, at last. . .

"Hey! I see light."

"You sure? Eyes can play tricks."

"No. For real! Light."

The crevice widened, and she scraped more quickly forward on bloodied hands and knees. Then she tumbled down into a larger space.

She was in an enormous dome-shaped room, with light pouring in from above. Ken appeared in the crevice, almost falling on her. "Air's better here. We can hold out awhile even if we can't get out."

Lupe glanced up at the hole in the roof, mesmerized by the sight of clear blue sky and white clouds moving across the opening. "That's big enough to squeeze through, don't you think?"

"Yeah, but it's at least twenty feet up, and nothing to climb on. Sorry, no way we can reach it. Not in a hundred years. Sorry, Lupe. We're still trapped."

Eventually, the others made it through the crevice into the larger, better ventilated room. Once their lungs were filled again, the five tried to come up with a plan. Still no phone service. No way to ignite a fire for smoke signals.

And then a voice floated eerily into the stone chamber. "Hello! Is anyone down there?"

"We're hallucinating," Maeve declared.

"No we're not. Hello up there!" Ken called.

A bushy head appeared in the hole, dark against the sky beyond it. *There's something familiar about that voice,* Lupe thought. "Joe, is that you?"

"Heh–heh," the homeless man cackled. "I was afraid you kids were done for. Just a minute, I have some climbing gear in my backpack."

The face disappeared and then a rope with knots at intervals dropped down to the floor. "I tied the other end to a boulder, so it should hold. Come on up."

One by one, they pulled themselves up the rope, through the hole, into glorious sunlight and freedom.

"Joe," asked Lupe, "how did you know we were in there?"

"I followed Mr. Fancy Pants," Joe replied. "Last week, he found the cave. After he left, I helped myself to some of those big old coins. Figure it's as much mine as his. Then today, I saw you kids go in, before he blew up the entrance. I remembered this hole. Always figured it led into the back of the same cave but didn't know for sure." He looked at Lupe. "Sorry I gave ya such a scare in the alley, little lady. Guess I got a bit greedy about the treasure."

"You aren't the only one." Lupe knew what greed felt like, she realized. None of them had been immune.

"How long ago did McGinnis leave?" Ken asked.

"He took a long, relaxed smoke after blasting the cave entrance. Seemed rather pleased with himself. Pulled out in his jeep just before I called down to ya."

"Maybe there's still time for the authorities to catch him." Ken grabbed his cell phone. "We got service now." He punched a button and quickly explained the situation to his father.

When he hung up, he didn't look happy. "The nearest police will take half an hour to get to the road. By that time, McGinnis will be through the loop and on his way to who knows where. Odds are good that creep is gonna get away."

"After what he did to us, I wanna' see him fry," Maeve snarled.

Lupe recalled Ms. Kwan's words on their first trip to the canyon: *It's important to note topography when looking at crime scenes, because victims and criminals all have to deal with the same barriers and access routes.* "Wait a minute—Joe, where are our horses?"

"Ran from the blast, but they're still grazin' not too far from the front of the cave."

Lupe pulled a crumpled map labeled Devil's Canyon Trail Guide from a pant pocket and quickly unfolded it. *Good thing I kept this from my hike with Ken,* she thought. "McGinnis has to follow the bottom of the arroyo in his jeep, then get on the road circling way around back to the freeway." Her finger traced along the map. "But there is a trail marked here that goes up over the canyon side and connects to the road. It's a good shortcut. We might be able to take it and reach the road before McGinnis. Only question is—can our horses make it over the canyon?"

Joe looked over her shoulder. "That trail starts 'bout a quarter mile from here. I've seen Peshlaki riding his horse on it."

"But what can we do if we get on the road ahead of McGinnis?" Ken asked. "He has a pretty nasty gun, remember?"

"There's a gate at this place here." Joe pointed to the map. "It's a narrow pass. Sometimes they shut the road for flooding. If you close that gate—"

"That might hold him 'til the police arrive," Ken finished. "Come on guys, let's saddle up."

After twenty minutes, and a ride that Lupe found exhilarating—though Wire and Maeve nearly fell off their horses several times—the five cantered down a trail onto the road. Just as Joe had said, to their right was a narrow pass between steep rock walls and a weather-beaten, metal gate hanging from one hinge.

"I'm guessing we're about five minutes ahead of that creep," Ken said.

They galloped to the gate and dismounted, then pushed at the heavy barrier. As the gate swung ponderously, squeaking loudly, Lupe noticed the large plate from the other hinge lying on the ground. She picked it up just as something went "*Zinngg!*" off the gate, just past Maeve's shoulder. They looked up the road at an open-top jeep, sun glinting off the gun in the driver's hand.

"Run for it—hide!" Ken shouted.

A second shot whizzed through the air by Lupe's head.

"Go, get outta here!"

Wire, Maeve, and Jessa sprinted for shelter behind boulders as Lupe helped Ken shut the gate and fasten the lock. Then they dashed after the others.

Lupe threw herself behind a rock formation that looked like an enormous thumb sticking up from the desert floor. She heard the screech of brakes, and peeked at the road. McGinnis stopped the jeep twenty feet away from the gate and jumped out. He glanced ahead past the obstruction, saw Lupe, and pulled his revolver.

Wham!

She pulled her head back just as a bullet shattered the rock beside her.

"You kids are amazing," the man yelled from the road. "Amazing pests!"

Pow!

Lupe wanted to see what was happening, but she was afraid to take another look.

Bam!

She slid her face just to the point where she could see around the rock. McGinnis had shot the lock open, and was kicking the gate aside.

He's going to get away. After all the misery he's caused, this monster is going to sip margaritas in the sun and live like a king. Lupe's breath came fast and hard. Before she could think, she stepped out from behind the rock, stood in the middle of the road, and waved her arms.

"Lupe!" Ken screamed. "Get back."

"Hey!" she yelled at McGinnis. "Want another notch on your gun?"

He looked at her with eyes like a lizard's.

"One more kill—that should satisfy your twisted need," she taunted.

His right arm with the heavy revolver went up slowly.

"I'll bet your own mother hated you—that's why you're such a sicko!"

McGinnis sighted along the long barrel.

Lupe closed her eyes. Waited. . . .

Boom!

It felt like a giant sledgehammer smashing her chest.

"Now!" she gasped to the others. "Get 'im! He's out of bullets."

And then she blacked out.

When she opened her eyes, Ken Benally was crouched beside, holding her hand. Lupe licked her dry lips, managed to speak. "Was anyone else counting?"

"You bet. I was praying for some way to make him fire that sixth shot, when you—Lupe, that was the most incredible thing I've ever seen. Maybe the most stupid too." His voice sounded shaky.

"M–McGinnis?"

"The others are tying him up now. He's not much of a fighter when his bullets are gone." Ken smiled down at her, but his lips trembled. "I thought you were dead."

Ken still held her left hand in his, and she managed a wan smile at him. She moved her right hand—it was lacerated in half-a-dozen places—and reached under her t-shirt, grasped the heavy hinge plate she'd picked up, and pulled it out. It felt so heavy. Ken took it from her limp fingers and held it up for her to see. The flattened slug was in the very center, forming a dent at least half an inch deep. *Thank God, the metal didn't break. Must be one nasty bruise, though.*

Maeve came over, crouched by Lupe's other side. "Wow. You got guts, Stick Girl."

Lupe managed a grin. "Thanks, Vampire Girl."

"Where'd you get that metal plate?"

"It was on the ground by the gate. I thought it might come in handy, so I grabbed it."

"What if he'd taken a head shot? You think about that before you did it?"

"Figured he'd be consistent. Remember how Ms. Kwan said the killer must have practiced heart shots? Besides…" Lupe inhaled and winced. "Clint Eastwood did this in an old Western. Worked for him."

Jessa and Wire joined Maeve beside Lupe. "We got him tied up good," the spectacled boy reported.

Jessa crouched beside Ken. "Lupe, thank heavens you're okay." She put her arm over Ken's shoulder. Instantly, he let go of Lupe's hand and hugged Jessa's waist.

Lupe sighed. *If this was a novel, I'd get the boy after taking a bullet. Reality sucks.*

She heard the throbbing *chop-chop-chop* of a helicopter overhead. "Here comes the cavalry," Wire said.

Lupe dropped her head back on the ground and closed her eyes. Her mind played the strange, whistling notes of an Ennio Morricone musical score.

That evening, Lupe waited alone in a doctor's office, bandages all over her arms and legs, and thick cloth wrappings around her torso, like a mummy. Her parents had offered to wait with her, but she wanted a few minutes alone. She felt as banged up emotionally as physically.

The doctor came into the room and handed Lupe an X-ray.

"What's this?"

"There's a crack in your sternum where the bullet impacted," the physician replied. "Not much you can do but wait for it to heal."

"Gonna hurt bad for a while, right?"

"I'm afraid so." The doctor paused a moment, looking at Lupe. She could see the kindness in her eyes.

"Is there something else?" Lupe asked.

"Yes, there is, if you're willing to talk about it." She put a hand on Lupe's arm. "How long have you been anorexic?"

Chapter 8
A BIGGER MYSTERY

A week later, CSC convened in Mr. Chesterton's science room.

Ms. Kwan began, "I hardly know what to say, after last week's . . . excitement. You were insanely irresponsible—crazy—to go off into danger without telling us. If you ever do anything so reckless again, this club is over. Understand?"

The students nodded.

"That being said, what you achieved was truly remarkable. You found the treasure and solved a murder case."

"It was your lessons in geographical mappings that showed us how to do it," Wire noted in a rare humble moment.

"Then—with a little help from a homeless good Samaritan," Ms. Kwan continued, "you escaped from a deadly trap and apprehended the murderer. Reckless, foolhardy—but amazing."

"Was the police department able to recover the treasure after taking McGinnis into custody?" Mr. Chesterton asked.

"We were. He was anxious to bargain, and he told us where to find a locked metal shed full of silver and gold packed in plastic containers, near the airfield where he meant to escape the country."

"So," Maeve was clearly excited, "we're rich? I mean, finders keepers, right?"

"No. Owners keepers. That treasure is claimed property."

"The bank?"

The detective shook her head. "Wish it were that simple. Pacific Coast Cattleman's Bank has, over the past century, divided into three separate entities. They all claim their right to the silver and gold. Having been hidden in the ground for a hundred years, I'm guessing that treasure will be tied up for another century in legal battles."

"Gee," Maeve reflected, "forget about crime scene work. I wanna be a lawyer."

A few days later, Lupe sat at the dinner table with her mom, dad, and little brother Hector.

"Lupe, eat your menudo."

She stared unhappily at the reddish soup. She thought about what she and the doctor had talked about. But she just wasn't hungry, and she didn't want to gain weight. . . .

"Jim from Karations called today," her father said.

"And?" Lupe's mom asked, putting down her spoon.

"They want me to move down there and start working for them right away. We'll put the house up for sale, and you three will join me soon as we have a buyer."

Lupe took a small sip of the spicy soup and looked at her parents. "We don't really have to move, you know."

"Sorry, *Mija*," her mom spoke gently, "but we can't afford to live here."

Lupe gave her parents a grin, then reached for her purse, pulled out a check, and handed it to her father. "Does this change things? You can do whatever you want with it."

Raul Arellano almost fell off his chair. "*Oye*, Lupe—where did you get this?"

"Ms. Kwan gave the two coins that Joe left for a tip back to me. Said the banks were grateful for my help and said I could keep them. So I took them downtown to the humismatist shop on Leroux Street and showed them to the store owner. He said an 1896 Morgan silver dollar, in mint condition, of that variety, is very rare—and then he offered a hundred grand for the pair."

Her parents shook their heads in wonder. Hector's eyes were round.

"I hate to say this, Lupe," her dad said slowly, "but don't you think you should let homeless Joe know the value of those coins? He needs that money worse than we do. I don't think he intended to give away a small fortune when he left you that tip."

"I told Joe. He has a dozen more of the silver dollars. He says he's thrilled to learn their value and hopes I can do some good with mine. The banks are letting him keep his as well."

Her father grinned and shook his head. "So Joe the homeless guy—"

"Will soon be one of the richest men in town."

"That should make things interesting," her dad mused.

"And it turns out Joe also paid two of the coins to Stanley Peshlaki for some tobacco. The medicine man is planning to open a small clinic near his Hogan, where Native people can receive traditional healing chants along with modern health care." Lupe took a big breath. "So . . . can we stay in Flagstaff?"

"Of course!" Her father gave her a hug.

Lupe leaned against him for a moment, then glanced at the clock. "Oh, hey, I gotta run to a meeting."

"Crime Scene Club meeting late?"

"No, it's another kind of group." She hesitated, then pulled a brochure out of her purse and set it on the table. Written across the front were the words Eating Disorders Anonymous.

Her mom's eyes glistened. "Lupe, I'm so proud of you. This means more to me than that check does."

Funny thing, Lupe thought as she walked into town. *As scary as it was back in the canyon, this meeting scares me even more. Seems the biggest mystery is learning to understand my own heart.*

FORENSIC NOTES

CRIME SCENE CLUB, CASE #1

Evidence List

Vocab Words

reverie
posse

Deciphering the Evidence

Just as she falls into a daydream Felicity was shaken out of her *reverie* by the train's sudden and violent halt.

The grey-eyed man tells Felicity that it will take half an hour to get a *posse* together to trail the train robbers. A posse is a group of people called together to help track down lawbreakers.

Evidence List #2

19th-Century Slang

The power and speed of early locomotives, or trains, inspired people to call them *iron horses*.

Felicity's train ride is like an adventure right out of the pages of a *dime novel*. Dime novels were melodramatic novels of romance and adventure that were popular in late 19th- and early 20th-century America.

Felicity overhears the bandits talking about one of their own who was shot, saying he would need mercy when he reaches the *pearly gates*. Pearly gates is an informal way of saying the gates of heaven; it comes from a biblical reference to heavenly gates made of pearl.

> *Fast Fact*
> The Pinkerton logo was an open eye surrounded by the motto, "We Never Sleep!" The term "private eye" was inspired by this logo.

One of the robbers orders the guards to "drop your *irons*," which is another way of saying "Drop your guns."

Who Were the Pinkertons?

Pinkerton is short for the Pinkerton National Detective Agency, which was the first private detective agency in the United States. Established by Allan Pinkerton in 1850, the Pinkertons specialized in the capture of counterfeiters and train robbers. In 1861 Allan Pinkerton uncovered a plot to assassinate Abraham Lincoln while he was en route to his inauguration. Pinkerton warned Lincoln and then safely escorted him through Baltimore at night. By the 1870s the Pinkertons had the world's largest collection of mug shots and a criminal database.

CHAPTER 1

Evidence List

Vocab Words

controversial
medicine man
noir
jeopardy
secure
perpetrator
monotone
oblivious

Deciphering the Evidence

Detective Kwan calls the Crime Scene Club a *controversial* experiment. The Detective is positive about the new club, but it may be causing arguments between her and others who do not think it is safe.

Stanley Peshlaki is a Navajo *medicine man* with knowledge of local plants and their healing properties. As a healer and spiritual guide for his Native American community, Mr. Peshlaki helps to promote harmony between humans and nature.

Jessa tells the other members of the Crime Scene Club that she applied to be in the club because of the "whole gritty *noir* thing." Noir is the French word for "black," and the way Jessa uses it is to suggest the mystery, darkness, and danger of the world of crime.

Jeopardy means danger, so it makes sense that the area where a criminal is mostly likely to be found based on the patterns and places of crimes is called the jeopardy surface.

To *secure* a crime site means to guard it from disturbance and protect anyone in the area from harm.

Mr. Chesterton explains to the club that when a *perpetrator* is finally brought to the courtroom, he won't be convicted on the basis of profiling. A perpetrator in this instance is someone who carries out or commits a crime.

When Wire introduces himself to the club, he speaks in a *monotone*, which means that his voice has a single tone—it does not go up or down in pitch.

When the students joke quietly among themselves, Mr. Chesterton continues with his lesson, *oblivious* to the whispers. He is not aware of or not paying attention to their side conversations.

What Is Navajo Nation?

Navajo Nation (Diné Bikéyah) is the homeland of the Navajo, or Diné, people. The Nation covers over 27,000 square miles (approximately 69,231 square kilometers) and extends into the states of Arizona, New Mexico and Utah. The Navajo Nation is the largest Indian Nation in North America, both in membership and landmass.

The World of Forensics

Our English word "forensic" comes from the Latin word *forensis*, which means "forum"—the public area where in the days of ancient Rome a person charged with a crime presented his case. Both the person accused of the crime and the accuser would give speeches presenting their sides of the story. The person with the best forensic skills usually won the case.

In the modern world, "forensics" has come to mean the various procedures, many of them scientific in nature, used to answer questions of interest to the legal system—usually, to solve a crime. Detective Kwan and the new members of the CSC will use many of these procedures in their cases. In this case, their first, the procedures involved with forensic mapping will prove to be particularly useful to them.

Who Is the Virgin of Guadalupe?

The Virgin of Guadalupe, also known as Our Lady of Guadalupe, is a Roman Catholic religious icon and an important symbol of Mexican identity. In the 16th century, the Virgin appeared in a vision to a poor Indian named Juan Diego. The Virgin's appearance to Juan Diego as one of his own people was significant in that it helped convert to vast numbers of Native Americans to Christianity.

Forensic Procedures Used in CSC Case #1

Geographical Profiling (Forensic Mapping)

Geographical profiling, sometimes called forensic mapping, uses a system of maps to predict the most likely location for a suspect's home, hideout, travel routes, work, or even the site of the suspect's next crime. How does a geographical profiler do this? As Detective Kwan explains, "You start with the crime scene, then work backward, using the linkage of crime location and physical boundaries to establish a jeopardy surface, revealing the criminal's residence or staging area for the crime." In other words, detectives take what they know about the suspect and the area surrounding the crime scene, and they use this information to try and guess more about the suspect.

It is not all guess work; geographical profilers gather a lot of information before creating a profile. The geographical profiler needs to be familiar with the case file and the crime scenes; she needs to conduct interviews with investigators and witnesses; she needs to study maps of the area; she needs to be familiar with the neighborhood demographics; and finally she needs to use computerized analysis programs. Predator, one of these computer analysis programs, is mentioned by Detective Kwan, but others include Criminal Geographic Targeting (CGT), Dragnet, and Crime Stat. After a profiler has combined all the information, she can use mathematical modeling to create a "geoprofile" of the suspect. In a case with no known suspect, this profile gives detectives a limited area within which to begin a search.

Crime Scene Reconstruction

A clear spatial record of the crime scene itself is also important to any investigation. Photography is a part of this, but the total station mentioned by Detective Kwan is another. The total station is a surveying instrument that uses a combination of a theodolite (an instrument that measures angles), a distance meter, and a computer. The station takes measurements and generates a map of a surveyed area. This information can be used in other analyses, such as ballistics or blood spatter. If it might be valuable to the case, a computerized version of the entire crime scene may be reconstructed.

Trace Evidence

Mr. C tells the Crime Scene Club that they will learn to secure a crime scene, touch nothing, and search for even the smallest traces of physical evidence: spilled fluids, drops of blood, flakes of metal. He knows that every person who is physically involved in a crime always—no matter how careful he or she may be—leaves some tiny trace evidence behind: a fingerprint, a fiber, a grain of sand. Seemingly insignificant things—tiny threads, hairs, dust, pollen, bits of metal and glass—can make all the difference when it comes to solving a crime.

1.1 Surveying instruments such as this total station can help investigators create a map of the crime scene. The total station is a measuring device that determines distances and angles. The collected measurements can then be downloaded to a computer where mapping software can reconstruct a crime scene. This method not only saves time with crime scenes that span great distances, but can prove safer in situations where the crime scene is dangerous for crime scene specialists.

CHAPTER 2

Evidence List

Vocab Words

topography
access
saboteurs
Hogan
acronym
coordinates
eccentric
contaminating
documentation
omission
technicality

Deciphering the Evidence

Detective Kwan stresses the importance of noting *topography* when looking at crime scenes. Topography refers to the natural or man-made features of an area, such as hills and valleys.

Victims and criminals all have to deal with the same barriers and *access* routes. An access route is a way of entering or exiting someplace.

The train robbery newspaper article reports that a section of rail was removed by *saboteurs*. A saboteur is someone who sabotages, or deliberately destroys property.

Stanley Peshlaki lives in a traditional *Hogan*. A Hogan is an eight-sided Navajo Indian dwelling, usually made of logs and mud.

Maeve has trouble understanding when Detective Kwan speaks "acronym." She is jokingly suggesting that *acronyms*, words formed from the first letters of a name, are a language all their own. Acronyms can also be abbreviations rather than words, such as ESDA for electrostatic detection apparatus, but these are more precisely called initialisms.

Detectives noted the GPS *coordinates* of the victim and the shooter in the Devil's Canyon incident. Coordinates, in this instance, refers to a set of numbers used to pinpoint a location.

Lupe thought that Joe, the homeless man who sometimes stopped at the coffee shop where she worked, acted *eccentric*, or in an odd manner.

The students learned how to walk carefully over a crime site to avoid *contaminating* it with footprints or by tramping over clues. Contaminating means causing something to be unclean, impure, or spoiled in some way by direct contact.

Detective Kwan tells the students that *documentation*, or organized records of detailed information, may be the most crucial part of an investigation.

One little *omission* in an investigation, that is, leaving something undone, such as failing to record a piece of evidence, could mean that a criminal walks free on a *technicality*.

A technicality is a detail that might seem insignificant but that is important, for instance, in a court of law.

Forensic Procedures Used in CSC Case #1

Forensic Photography

Using photographs to document evidence is important for many types of cases. The photographs can be used to simply record the surrounding conditions and evidence at the time of the crime—but they can also be taken back to the lab, where computers are used to enhance details on the photographs that might not otherwise be discernable to the human eye.

Recent advances in digital imaging have greatly improved many aspects of forensic photography. Digital techniques allow detectives and the lab technicians who help them to capture, edit, output, and transfer images faster than they could with processed film. In the old days, when photographers depended on darkrooms, many techniques had to be applied through time-consuming trial and error; now, with digital photography, these techniques can be instantly applied on a computer, and the results are immediately visible on the monitor.

Besides the advantages of speed and efficiency, digital photography also offers some techniques that were never available using traditional photography. One forensic photography technique, for example, is the ability to correct the perspective of an image. As long as the photograph contains a scale of reference, it is possible to take an image that was shot at an incorrect angle and correct it so that the scale is the same across the plane of focus.

Recent technology also allows GPS coordinates to be combined with photographs taken on a digital camera. This is particularly useful when using forensic mapping techniques.

Maintaining Chain of Custody

The chain of custody of evidence is the record of every person who has come into contact with that evidence. In a criminal case, the fewer people who handle the evidence the better, but if evidence must be handled, there are particular procedures that must be followed to preserve any trace evidence, fingerprints, or DNA evidence that may be present. When Stanley Peshlaki hands Detective Kwan the threatening note, she is careful to put on latex gloves before accepting it from him. She does so because the latex gloves protect the note from contamination from her skin oils, dirt, and her own DNA.

In maintaining the chain of custody it is also vital to keep a clear written record of exactly where and when individuals did come into contact with the evidence. After all, on a crime scene investigation, if an agent finds a piece of evidence, someone will have to pick it up eventually. The evidence needs to be packed and transported for secure storage or additional testing in a laboratory. Therefore, after she is finished reviewing the note, Detective Kwan stores it in a protective evidence bag and then carefully labels it with a permanent marker. Eventually, documents can include information such as the name/initials of the individual collecting the evidence; each person who subsequently touched the evidence; dates the items were collected and then transferred from person to person; from where the item(s) were collected; agency and case number; the victim's or suspect's name; and a brief description of the item.

Fingerprints

Fingerprints are defined by unique patterns of ridges on the fingers. There are three basic types of fingerprints: visible prints, such as those made in ink, paint, or blood; invisible, or latent, prints, which can only be seen using certain techniques; and plastic prints, which are made by touching something soft, such as wax. A fingerprint can be made even when there are no substances such as paint or soft wax simply from sweat mixed with the body's amino acids. Amazingly, scientists have now developed ways to lift fingerprints off human skin.

When a person touches a piece of paper, moisture, water, and some proteins from the skin get deposited on the surface and then dry. These invisible prints can then be made visible using developing agents that react with the organic matter in the skin secretions. These agents can be applied by immersing the prints in liquids, but they are more commonly applied through indirect means such as sprays or gases. In fact, fuming with Super Glue is the most common method of developing latent prints. The chemicals in the fumes stick the amino acids in the print and build up a white substance. This can be photographed directly or treated with a colored powdered and then collected.

Hairs and Fibers

On average, a person loses between 50 and 100 hairs from the scalp each day. It is no wonder, then, that Detective Kwan wants to analyze Mr. Peshlaki's note for hair and fiber evidence, both of which are types of trace evidence.

Not only the suspect leaves hair at the crime scene; any victim(s), witnesses, detectives, or even pets that pass through may drop a few hairs to confuse the issue. This is why all hair samples should be carefully collected at every crime scene. Each collected hair will then need to be carefully packaged and labeled.

Age and sex cannot always be determined from hair examination, but certain markers may provide indicators. Infants generally have finer hair, while the elderly undergo pigment loss and variations in hair shaft diameter, which can be seen on microscopic examination. Longer, treated (dyed) hairs are more often found in female hairs. DNA testing can definitively determine sex from a hair sample, but this is not routinely done.

Fiber and thread evidence is similar to hair evidence in how it is handled and examined by crime scene investigators. Fiber samples are units of textile material that may be natural plant fibers (cotton, linen, sisal, hemp), natural animal fibers (sheep's wool, alpaca wool, cashmere), or man-made fibers (polyester, nylon, acrylics). The type of fiber will be important for a number of reasons. Certain fabrics will tear and transfer more easily than others, so if there are many fibers from a fabric that is not shed easily, a detective might surmise the cloth was torn forcibly. Also the fiber type can be compared to the fiber type of the suspect's clothes. Rare fiber types may help narrow down suspects.

Fibers can be transferred from or to the clothing of a suspect, and from or to a source such as a bed, carpet, curtain, or other source at a crime scene. Fibers and threads are also easily caught on sharp objects, such as broken windows, ripped screens, or the spine of a small cactus. Just as with hair evidence, the crime scene must be thoroughly examined and cleaned of any fiber evidence. As Detective Kwan did, fibers should be removed using tweezers and then carefully bagged and labeled for testing. The type, number, color, and location of the fibers (on specific parts of the body or in certain areas of the crime scene) should also be recorded.

Blood Traces and Blood Spatter

Any blood evidence at a crime scene must Blood trace evidence can also be used to help determine the location of a crime or the orientation of a suspect during a shooting. Though Shadow's body is gone, the Crime Scene Club can find the traces of dried blood on the ground to locate where the dog was shot. By examining the direction of the blood spatter, they may even be able to figure out where the shot came from.

Interpreting blood spatter involves biology, chemistry, physics, and math skills. The velocity or energy of the blood spatter determines the size of the blood drops; a high energy impact, such as a bullet, causes small drops. The shape of the blood drops indicates the impact angle. Once this angle has been determined, the point of origin (assuming a flat, hard landing surface) can

2.1 Blood drops have a spherical shape when moving through the air. When blood lands on a flat surface, the diameter of the blood in flight is equal to width of the spatter. Basic facts about blood and blood spatter behavior can help investigators calculate the point of origin of the blood or the cause of the spatter, such as, a gunshot, beating or stabbing.

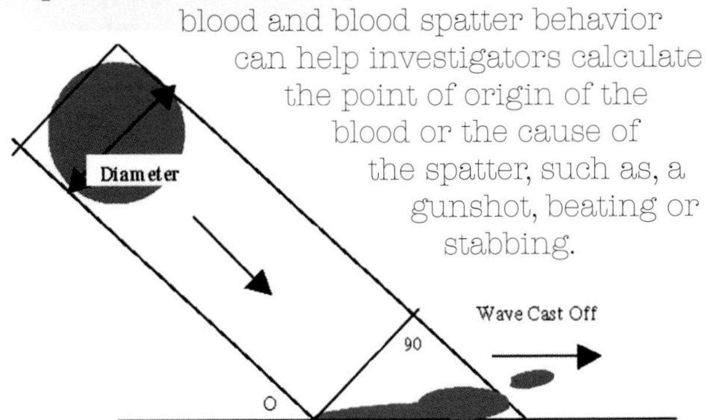

be found using a spatter computer program. When the blood spatter is not on a flat surface, more variables must be entered to determine the point of origin.

Global Positioning Satellite Receiver

The Global Positioning System (GPS) was developed by the U.S. Department of Defense, using a constellation of satellites circling the Earth to transmit precise microwave signals to GPS receivers that allow users to determine exact locations, time, speed, and distances. When this information is combined with digital photography, the location coordinates (longitude and latitude) can be embedded on the photographs like a date stamp. This means the location can be exactly placed on a map.

Quick Reminder

The lines of longitude and latitude allow human beings to know exactly where they are on the planet. Longitude lines run north to south (but measure east and west), starting at 0° at the Prime Meridian in Greenwich, England, and progressing to 180° eastward and –180° westward. Lines of latitude run east to west (and measure north and south), starting at 0° at the Equator and going to 180° at the Earth's poles.

CHAPTER 3

Evidence List

Vocab Words

scrutinize
disembodied
fetid

Deciphering the Evidence

Lupe sits down at a table to *scrutinize*—or closely examine—the coin given to her by Joe, the homeless man.

When Lupe encounters Joe in the dark alley, she can't see him very well, and his *disembodied* voice makes her skin crawl with goose bumps. It is as if he is just a voice without a physical body.

When Joe pulls her down to the pavement, Lupe chokes on his foul-smelling, or *fetid*, breath.

The Thrill of Crime Solving

Why does Lupe question Joe alone when she knows it is dangerous? Why do so many of our television shows revolve around criminal investigations? The answer to both questions may lie in the fact that as a culture we seem to be obsessed with crime and crime solving. At the heart of this obsession may

3.1 Spectators gathered at the Roman coliseum to watch gladiators battle to the death.

be the thrill Detective Kwan warned the club about, the thrill the Lupe recognizes as she enters the dark alley.

Human interest in horrific crimes and human brutality is not a new phenomenon: Roman gladiator contests filled stadiums and medieval crowds flocked to public hangings. However, in addition to this morbid interest, people are innately curious. People love to solve mysteries, and it is easy to get carried away looking for clues, especially as each new piece of the puzzle falls into place.

Detective Kwan even suggests a similarity between the rush of finding a vital clue and the effect of drugs on the brain. Drugs alter brain chemistry, creating a high, or rush of positive feeling through the body. If the drug is taken regularly enough, eventually the body has trouble functioning without the presence of the drug within the bloodstream. When the body reaches this stage, the person has an addiction. People form addictions to things other than drugs: food, gambling—and perhaps crime solving.

CHAPTER 4

Evidence List

Vocab Words

tangible
court order
trajectory
unsentimental

Deciphering the Evidence

Detective Kwan explains to the club that *tangible* evidence and *court orders* are necessary to take any action against a crime suspect. Tangible in this case means the evidence is concrete enough to be treated as fact. A court order is an order from a court that requires a person either to do or to stop doing something.

After a tourist was grazed by a bullet, investigators used a triple-mounted laser to trace the bullet's *trajectory*. Trajectory is the path that something takes through space, such as a bullet or a blood spatter.

Wire argues with Jessa that they must use *unsentimental* logic to solve crimes. Even though they like Mr. Peshlaki, they need to remain tough-minded when considering whether he might be a suspect.

Forensic Procedures Used in CSC Case #1

Fiber Analysis

Fibers are not unique like fingerprints or DNA, so they do not provide the same evidence to identify a suspect. What fiber evidence can do is to tie a suspect to crime scene as well as provide clues about the suspect—in this case socioeconomic status and gender.

When looked at from far away, the small blue threads from the cactus might all look the same, but when examined under a microscope, differences became apparent. The fiber analyst probably first compared shape, color, size (diameter), and microscopic appearance to help determine the type of fibers. In this case, the fibers were a mix of a natural fiber (wool) and a synthetic fiber. This kind of fabric blend is commonly seen in men's suit

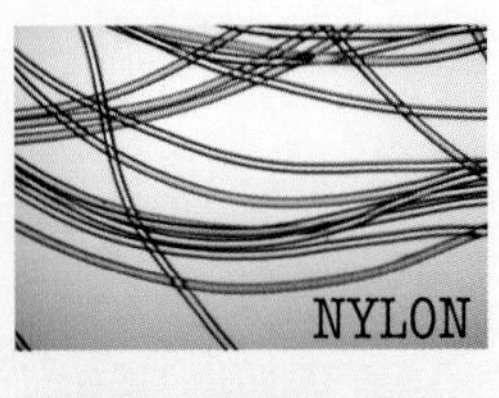

4.1. Fiber analysts can determine the type of fibers found at a crime scene by magnifying them. These images show the contrasts between animal fibers such as wool and synthetic or man-made fiber like nylon. Fiber evidence can be crucial in placing a suspect at the scene of a crime. For example, if particular fibers are found at a crime scene and match the clothing fabric of the suspect, it may mean that the fiber was transferred during the crime.

jackets. Detective Kwan notes that the fibers probably came from an "expensive" man's suit jacket, possibly because of the fineness of the wool fibers. In addition, the particular type of blue dye might indicate the cost of the suit from which the fibers tore. The fiber analyst would have found the chemical composition of the blue dye by separating the dye into its parts using chromatography.

Ballistics

The study of movements and forces involved in the propulsion of objects through the air is known as ballistics. Ballistics can be applied to any object moving through the air, but forensic ballistics is most commonly associated with bullets. A bullet has a high amount of energy when it leaves the barrel of a gun. As it travels, this energy decreases, until eventually the bullet drops to the ground. The factors in between the time the bullet was fired and when it hit the ground are what a forensic ballistics expert must take into account when trying to determine a shooter's location. How far did the bullet travel? What did it hit along the way?

Alibis

An alibi is the plea or defense by which a suspect will attempt to prove he is not guilty because he was somewhere else. The word also commonly refers to a person who will vouch for your whereabouts at a certain time and place.

CHAPTER 5

Evidence List

Vocab Words

evasive
speculation
MO
hoodoos
escalating
simulation

Deciphering the Evidence

Lupe tells Mr. Chesterton that she thinks Arnold Huston is suspect, because he was being *evasive* when questioned. She thought he was trying to avoid answering the investigators' questions.

The discussion among the teenagers was dominated by *speculation* about the murder. They had forgotten for the moment about the girls' fight and were more interested in thinking and talking about the latest news in the case.

Detective Kwan tells the class that the *MO* of the perpetrator who shot Arnold Huston appeared to be that of a sniper. MO stands for *modus operandi* and it refers to the way an act is carried out. An easy way to remember it is to think "mode of operation."

In between the place where Feesham was wounded and the point where Huston was murdered, there are hundreds of boulders, rockslides, *hoodoos*, juniper, and piñon trees. A hoodoo is a column of oddly shaped rock, carved that way by forces of nature such as wind and rain.

Detective Kwan informs the students that they will keep several teams patrolling the area of the crime, due to the pattern of *escalating* behavior. The investigator is concerned about the increasing number of incidents.

Wire tells Ken that online role playing games are a perfect *simulation* for a situation like the case they are involved in. Simulation is the act of re-creating a situation, a place, or an activity in a way that makes the experience as real as possible.

Forensic Procedures Used in CSC Case #1

Forensic Photography

It is vital to have a clear record of the crime scene. Going through and carefully collecting evidence is important, and documenting the scene through photography is the first part of the evidence collection.

The slides that Detective Kwan shows the Crime Scene Club were taken by the crime scene photographer. These images may be called on as evidence if the case goes to court. When photographs are used as evidence, they must be accurate and unaltered.

Digital images have a time and date stamp, which authenticates when they were taken. In addition, scales and contextual evidence will provide proof that the image is accurate. As with any evidence, maintaining the chain of custody through proper handling and labeling will prove that the images are unaltered.

What Does a Coroner Do?

A coroner is a public official who investigates and determines the cause of death, especially in cases when the death is not due to natural causes.

Powder Marks

When a gun is fired, pieces of unburned gunpowder are ejected from the barrel. These fragments do not travel far, but if they encounter an object along the way, they leave unique burn marks. Thre shape and pattern of powdermarks depend on the shooter's distance. A person who is shot at close range will show marks in a "stippling" pattern. Mr. Huston has no powder marks on his body, so the detectives are able to determine that the shooter was some distance away.

Bullet Identification

Bullet identification includes identifying the type of ammunition, the type of gun

Where Are the Ventricles and Sternum?

The ventricles and the sternum refer to parts of the anatomy of the chest. The sternum is the bone that can be felt at the midline of the chest between the ribs. It is more commonly known as the breast bone. The ventricles are parts of the human heart. The heart is composed of four chambers: an upper right side, a lower right side, an upper left side and a lower left side. The ventricles are the two lower chambers.

and the bullet manufacturer. If the bullet is found, the bullet manufacturer is relatively easy to determine, as most bullets have a unique company mark. Gun type can also be identified by examining the marks left on the bullet and casings; the metal of the bullet gets worn by the harder metal of the gun barrel. Most of this information is held in computer databases that are networked nationally, making it relatively easy to match the marks on a bullet from a crime scene to marks in a database.

Establishing Time of Death

Establishing the time that has passed since death occurred is also known as the postmortem interval (PMI). Estimates of the PMI are not perfect, but they provide a window of time that may rule out some suspects (or incriminate others). Techniques used to determine the time of death include rate of cooling, stiffening, pooling of blood at lowest body points, decomposition, and stomach contents. Algor mortis, the reduction of body temperature following death is usually a steady process that occurs at a rate of about 1–1.5 degrees per hour. Since the body had only cooled about three degrees, the Flagstaff PD could place the victim's death at two to three hours before the body was found. Rigor mortis, or the stiffening of the body that occurs after death, usually begins within two to six hours of death. This, combined with the cooling of the body, brought the coroner to the conclusion of about two hours since the time of death. In this case, the victim was found within hours of the murder. When more than a few hours have passed, other methods are used to estimate PMS.

Tire Track Identification

Casts of the tracks are made by filling in the impressions with a casting medium, most commonly dental stone, although plaster of Paris is still sometimes used. In a soft material, like the sandy soil in the arroyo, a frame is erected around the tire tracks before the cast is created. The dental stone may be drizzled in with a spoon or carefully piped in from the corner of a bag. Either way, the caster starts at the outer edges and moves in, being careful to work slowly to fill in every crevice so as to preserve details. Once the cast is dry, it can be lifted carefully from the edges of the frame.

Fast Fact

Plaster of Paris used to be the casting medium of choice for collecting track evidence. Dental stone is preferred now because it catches finer details, doesn't require a reinforcing material and is strong enough withstand cleaning.

Even if the tires themselves are not helpful, the distance between the tire marks may be. Careful examination of the photographs taken of the tracks may help determine the type of vehicle and whether it is four-wheel, two-wheel, or all-wheel drive.

How Do Lava Caves Form?

Most lava caves, or tubes, form when lava runs down the sides of a volcano. As the lava flows, the upper layers cool more quickly than the layers beneath the surface. Eventually, the molten lava stops flowing, leaving a hollow tube behind.

CHAPTER 6

Evidence List

Vocab Words

equestrians
scrutinized
desiccated
sardonic

Deciphering the Evidence

Jessa, Lupe, and Ken are experienced *equestrians*, which makes them more comfortable horseback riders than the other teens in the group.

When Jessa comments that the giant stone near the edge of the ravine feels funny, like paint, Lupe walks over to *scrutinize*, or closely examine, the boulder herself.

The teens discover a startling sight beside the mouth of the cave: a skeleton with its dried out, *desiccated* ribs and skull facing the ceiling. Desiccated means dried out.

As Lupe begins to put the pieces of the puzzle together in the cave with Mr. McGinnis, a *sardonic* smile flashes across the man's face. Sardonic means sneering, sarcastic, or mocking.

What Is a Buntline Special?

The Colt Buntline Special is a single-action revolver commissioned by Dime novelist Ned Buntline in 1876. In a single-action revolver the trigger only releases the hammer; to fire again the hammer must be manually cocked. The Buntline Special had a long twelve-inch barrel and carried .45 Long Colt ammunition. Modifications requested by Buntline the gun better precision and range.

Criminals and Technology

Computers and technology are an integral part of our world. We use cell phones, digital cameras, computers, and other technology daily. This is true as much for criminals as it is for law-abiding citizens. Technology used in crime scene investigation has increased dramatically in recent years as well. It can give detectives the sense that they have an advantage over the criminals they are chasing. However, as Lupe realizes in the cave, the bad guys have the same technology as the good guys!

Evidence List

mesmerized lacerated

Deciphering the Evidence

As she gazed through the hole in the roof of the dome-shaped room, Lupe is *mesmerized* by the sight of clear blue sky and white clouds. She is hypnotized or spellbound by the promising view of the outside world.

Lupe escapes serious injury by protecting her body with the iron plate she found in the cave, but her right hand is *lacerated*—or jaggedly cut—in half a dozen places.

> *Fast Fact*
> Ennio Morricone is an Academy Award-winning composer most famous for writing the soundtracks for Westerns.

What Is Anorexia?

Anorexia nervosa is an eating disorder characterized by extremely low body weight and a distorted body image. An individual with anorexia will deny herself food to the point of starvation because the reflection she sees in the mirror is overweight, even though in reality she is severely underweight.

CHAPTER 8

Evidence List

Vocab Words

convened
menudo
numismatist

Deciphering the Evidence

A week after the incident at the cave, Crime Scene Club *convened* in Mr. Chesterton's science room. This means that they gathered together for a meeting.

A few days after the CSC meeting, Lupe is sitting with her family at the dinner table for a meal of *menudo*, a hearty, spicy Mexican soup.

Lupe takes the coins that Detective Kwan returns to her to a *numismatist* shop. Numismatics refers to the collecting or selling of coins and other forms of currency.

Figure of Speech

Detective Kwan refers to homeless Joe as a *good Samaritan* for helping the teens escape from a deadly trap. The term "good Samaritan" comes from a story in the New Testament of the Bible in which a Samaritan, or resident of Samaria, is the only one who stops to help a man who has been beaten and robbed. This can be considered a figure of speech because Joe is not literally a Samaritan, but his actions resemble those of the individual in the Bible story. We use the term "good Samaritan" to refer to a compassionate person who unselfishly helps others.

Wrapping Up CSC Case #1

The members of the CSC got carried away on their first case. They were irresponsible and nearly paid the price for their recklessness. However, they also solved the case, found the treasure and helped to apprehend a murderer. This first case showed them by example that each aspect of the crime scene investigation—from simple collection of trace evidence to complicated mapping programs—is important for solving the case in the end. In the same way, every member of the team plays a role in solving the case, bringing different, but equally important skills to the investigation.

FURTHER READING

Craig, Emily. *Teasing Secrets from the Dead. My Investigations at America's Most Infamous Crime Scenes*. New York, NY: Crown Publishers, 2004.

Ferllini, Roxana. *Silent Witness. How Forensic Anthropology is Used to Solve the World's Toughest Crimes*. Buffalo, NY: Firefly Books, 2002.

Innes, Brian. *Forensic Science.* Philadelphia, PA: Mason Crest Publishers, 2006.

FOR MORE INFORMATION

Crime Library
www.trutv.com/library/crime/criminal_mind/profiling/geographic/7.html

How Stuff Works, "How Crime Scene Investigation Works, www.howstuffworks.com/csi.htm

BIBLIOGRAPHY

Genge, N. E. *The Forensic Casebook*. New York: Ballantine Books, 2004.

Lyle, D.P. *Forensics for Dummies*. Indianapolis, IN: Wiley Publishing Inc, 2004.

Owen, David. *Hidden Evidence. Forty True Crimes and How Forensic Science Helped Solved Them*. Buffalo, NY: Firefly Books, 2000.

Ramsland, Katherine. "Geographic Profiling." www.trutv.com/library/crime/criminal_mind/profiling/geographic/3.html

Rich, Tom, and Shivley, Michael, PhD. "A Methodology for Evaluating Geographic Profiling Software." Abt Associates, Inc, 2004.

Royal Canadian Mounted Police. "Geographic Profiling." www.rcmp-grc.gc.ca/techops/geog_prof_e.htm

Wecht, Cyril H. *Crime Scene Investigation.* Pleasantville, NY: The Reader's Digest Association, Inc, 2004.

INDEX

PICTURE CREDITS

2.1 FBI Law Enforcement Bulletin, p. 123
iStock.com
    4.1 Nehring, Nancy, p. 128
Jupiter Images
    3.1 p. 126
1.1 Schester, Stephen , SRA USAF, p. 115

To the best knowledge of the publisher, all images not specifically credited are in the public domain. If any image has been inadvertently uncredited, please notify Harding House Publishing Service, Vestal, New York 13850, so that credit can be given in future printings.

BIOGRAPHIES

Author

Kenneth McIntosh is a freelance writer and college instructor who lives in beautiful Flagstaff, Arizona (while CSC is fictional, Flagstaff is definitely real). He has enjoyed crime fiction—from Sherlock Holmes to CSI and Bones—and is thankful for the opportunity to create his own detective stories. Now, if he could only find his car keys . . .

Ken would like to thank the following people:
Tom Oliver, who invented the title 'Crime Scene Club' on a tram en route to the Getty Museum, and cooked up the best plots while we sat at his Tiki bar . . . Mr. Levin's Creative Writing students at the Flagstaff Arts and Leadership Academy, *who vetted the books . . . Rob and Jenny Mullen and Victor Viera, my Writer's Group, who shared their lives and invaluable insights . . . My recently deceased father, Dr. A Vern McIntosh, who taught me when I was a child to love written words. This series could not have happened without all of you.*

Series Consultant

Carla Miller Noziglia is Senior Forensic Advisor, Tanzania, East Africa, for the U.S. Department of Justice, International Criminal Investigative Training Assistant Program. A Fellow of the American Academy of Forensic Sciences her work has earned her many honors and commendations, including Distinguished Fellow from the American Academy of Forensic Sciences (2003) and the Paul L. Kirk Award from the American Academy of Forensic Sciences Criminalistics Section. Ms. Noziglia's publications include *The Real Crime Lab* (coeditor, 2005), *So You Want to be a Forensic Scientist* (coeditor 2003), and contributions to *Drug Facilitated Sexual Assault* (2001), *Convicted by Juries, Exonerated by Science: Case Studies in the Use of DNA* (1996), and the *Journal of Police Science* (1989).

Illustrator

Justin Miller first discovered art while growing up in Gorham, ME. He developed an interest in the intersection between science and art at the University of New Hampshire while studying studio art and archaeology. He applies both degrees in his job at the Public Archaeology Facility at Binghamton University. He also enjoys playing soccer, hiking, and following English Premier League football.